Heart & Soul

D0591492

COMING IN SUMMER 2000:

The Diaries
a Clearwater Crossing Special Edition

clearwater crossing

Heart & Soul

laura peyton roberts

BANTAM BOOKS
NEW YORK • TORONTO • LONDON • SYDNEY • AUCKLAND

RL 5.8, age 12 and up
HEART & SOUL
A Bantam Book / June 1998

All scripture quotations, unless otherwise indicated, are taken from
the HOLY BIBLE, NEW INTERNATIONAL VERSION®. NIV®.
Copyright © 1973, 1978, 1984 by International Bible Society. Used
by permission of Zondervan Publishing House. All rights reserved.

All rights reserved.
Copyright © 1998 by Laura Peyton Roberts.
Cover photography by Michael Segal.
Cover art copyright © 1998 by Bantam Doubleday Dell
Books for Young Readers.
No part of this book may be reproduced or transmitted
in any form or by any means, electronic or mechanical,
including photocopying, recording, or by any information
storage and retrieval system, without permission in
writing from the publisher.

If you purchased this book without a cover you should be aware
that this book is stolen property. It was reported as "unsold and
destroyed" to the publisher, and neither the author nor the
publisher has received any payment for this "stripped book."

ISBN 0-553-57124-9

Published simultaneously in the United States and Canada.

Bantam Books are published by Bantam Books, a division of Bantam
Doubleday Dell Publishing Group, Inc. Its trademark, consisting of the
words "Bantam Books" and the portrayal of a rooster, is Registered in
U.S. Patent and Trademark Office and in other countries. Marca Reg-
istrada. Bantam Books, 1540 Broadway, New York, New York 10036.

PRINTED IN THE UNITED STATES OF AMERICA

10 9 8 7 6

For Lindsay

For wisdom will enter your heart, and knowledge will be pleasant to your soul.

One

Everything was dark. Warm, soft darkness lay across Melanie like a blanket, blocking out the world. There wasn't any pain, there was nothing to worry about. She was floating. She was drifting. She was safe.

Nothing reached her. From time to time she caught a snatch of garbled conversation or became dimly aware of a light behind the darkness, but those things were of no importance. They couldn't touch her. She was somewhere else.

Perhaps she was dying, she thought. Surprisingly, the notion held no terror. An incredible calm had enveloped her, and she felt sure that whatever happened would be all right. She could even see a certain goodness in slipping out of life this way, quietly, totally at peace. If that was her fate, she didn't mind.

She didn't even mind that she was alone. She didn't *feel* alone. That was the strangest thing of all. She felt almost as if someone she knew were with her in that darkness, someone who loved her. . . .

"Watch out!" Jesse Jones cried, leaning on the horn and swerving his red BMW around an elderly couple in the crosswalk. "Get out of the way, why don't you?"

"Stop it, Jesse!" Nicole Brewster protested loudly. "What are you doing?"

Jesse glanced at her and Ben Pipkin in the rearview mirror, impatient with Nicole's backseat driving. "They're just standing in the middle of the road!" he shouted, not slowing in the slightest as he careened through the hospital parking lot on his way to the main entrance.

"They were *crossing* the road, Jesse," Jenna Conrad corrected quietly from the passenger seat. Her voice trembled slightly, and Jesse's stomach clenched even tighter with fear and apprehension.

Jesse had been in the gym when he'd heard the shrill of a siren. He'd run up to the access road behind the cafeteria just in time to see the ambulance streak out of the quad, lights flashing. Somehow, he'd known. Something in the pit of his stomach had balled up like a fist, and the sick, strange adrenaline of fear had flooded his bloodstream. He'd known, but he hadn't wanted to believe it.

Running to the fringe of the crowd of spectators, Jesse had grabbed the first kid he could reach.

"Who's in the ambulance?" he'd demanded, spinning him around. "Who got hurt?"

"Melanie Andrews," the boy had responded eagerly. "Man, you missed it. She was doing that flip thing onto the pyramid and she fell off backwards. You could hear her head crack clear across the quad."

Jesse had pushed him away and stumbled into the thickest part of the milling throng, looking for Wildcats. His football friends had been at the front of the crowd when he'd left the lunchtime spirit rally—one of them must have seen the whole thing. Or maybe he could find one of the cheerleaders, he'd thought. They'd know how badly Melanie was hurt.

"Jesse!" Ben had called, running up behind him. "Jesse, what happened? I was out on the soccer fields."

"Melanie fell. I didn't see it either," Jesse had answered brusquely. Then he'd spotted Jenna and Nicole talking urgently at the edge of the quad, their expressions worried. "Jenna!" he'd cried, waving. "Over here!"

She'd come pushing through the crowd to meet him halfway, Nicole right behind her.

"Melanie's unconscious and her head's bleeding. They took her to the hospital and Peter went with her," Jenna had said, not wasting a word. "Nicole and I want to go too, but we don't have a car and we can't find Leah or Miguel. Will you drive us?"

"Let's go!" Jesse had turned immediately toward the student parking lot and started to run. The four of them had piled into his car and pulled out with the tires screeching, leaving a stench of scorched rubber in their wake. None of them had said a word about the classes they'd miss or the demerits they'd get. All they wanted was to get to the hospital as quickly as possible.

"There! Park there!" Ben shouted suddenly. The hospital parking lot was nearly full, but a car was about to pull out of a space just ahead.

"Come on," Jesse muttered as the driver took her sweet time buckling her seat belt and backing up the car. "Come on, let's go!"

He put his head out the window. "Go, go, *go!*" he shouted, punching his horn. The woman turned her head to glare at him but finally drove out of his way. Jesse shot into the parking space, slammed on the brakes, and bolted out of the car in one fluid motion. Not waiting for the others, he raced across the blacktop toward the glass entry doors and burst through them with the strength of panic, charging into the lobby.

Peter Altmann looked up, startled by the commotion. He was sitting in a cheap plastic chair against the wall, and the expression in his eyes scared Jesse more than anything he'd heard about

Melanie's accident. "How's she doing?" he demanded. "Where is she?"

"She's still unconscious and they won't let me see her," Peter answered. "All we can do now is pray."

"Bull," Jesse retorted. "I'm going to see her."

"They won't let you," Peter insisted. "It's not going to help if you make a scene."

"We'll see," Jesse muttered, starting for the reception desk just as the glass doors opened again and Jenna, Ben, and Nicole came rushing in.

"How is she?" they asked worriedly.

Peter shook his head, then turned to Jesse. "You're going to get us all thrown out of here," he warned. "Even if they let you see her, what good can you do her right now?"

Jesse hesitated. It was a good question. In fact, he was probably the last person Melanie wanted to see.

"I just . . ." *want to be sure it wasn't my fault*, he finished silently. If only he and Melanie hadn't had that stupid fight right before she fell! *She didn't really mean those things she said to me*, he reassured himself, but the thought failed to soothe him. How could he be sure after the obnoxious way he'd behaved following Friday's football game?

What had he been thinking, anyway, trying to blackmail her into kissing him by pretending he knew something incriminating about her past? Anyone as hot as Melanie had to have *something* to hide, he'd figured then, thinking he must be a genius. In

5

retrospect, it seemed like the stupidest idea he'd ever had.

Still, he had *tried* to apologize. If he was willing to forget that she'd slapped his face, what did she have to hold a grudge about? She'd seemed pretty fired up when she'd told him off before the rally, though. *Could being angry with me have had anything to do with her falling?* The mere possibility made him weak with guilt.

"Peter!" Jenna said impatiently. "Tell us how she is!"

"I still don't know," Peter said as Jesse sank into a chair.

Peter's right. Throwing my weight around is probably pointless, Jesse realized. Not only that, but he was starting to think he might not be too well received if he succeeded. Jesse listened with only a fraction of his attention as Peter filled everyone in on the few details he had: Melanie had never regained consciousness in the ambulance, the doctors hadn't told him anything since they'd arrived, and no one was allowed to see her.

Jesse was so absorbed in his own worried thoughts that he barely noticed the lobby doors opening again, or a pale, disheveled man hurrying toward the reception desk.

"I'm Clay Andrews," the man announced in a low, anxious voice. "My daughter's school called and said there'd been an accident. Melanie Andrews—how is she?"

The receptionist snapped to attention. "Oh, Mr. Andrews! Dr. Levenstein wants to see you right away. Follow me, please." She left her desk to lead him down the corridor, her white nurse's shoes squeaking on the linoleum as Mr. Andrews shuffled silently behind her.

Jesse watched, amazed, as the man's slight back disappeared. *That* was Melanie Andrews's father? He'd expected Melanie's father to be larger than life—like Melanie herself—but the guy who'd just slunk down the hall was probably the least imposing person Jesse had ever seen. The rumpled shirt and khakis he wore looked as if they'd been plucked from a laundry hamper, and his shoulders were stooped like an old man's.

"Did you see that?" Jesse demanded as soon as Mr. Andrews was out of earshot. "Did you see Melanie's dad?"

"He's not exactly the way I pictured him," Ben ventured, apparently going for understatement.

"To say the least!" Jesse exclaimed. "All I can say is, she must take after her mother."

"Give him a break," said Peter. "Imagine how worried he must be."

"We're *all* worried," Jenna put in. "I wish they'd tell us if she's okay."

Ben nodded. "This is getting scary."

7

Jesse forgot about Mr. Andrews as the seriousness of Melanie's condition rushed back to him.

Please, God, he prayed, something he hadn't done for a while. *Please don't let me be responsible for this.*

"Aw, come on, Leah," Miguel del Rios cajoled as the two of them reached the edge of campus. "How many times do I have to say I'm sorry?"

Leah Rosenthal shrugged noncommittally. "I'll let you know when you get there."

Miguel had taken her off campus for lunch to make up for missing brunch with her parents on Sunday, but Leah was still annoyed with him, and she wasn't getting over it. She'd barely said a thing all through the meal. Now they were on their way to fifth-period biology, and Miguel was working overtime to put the incident behind him.

"It's not my fault my car broke down," he insisted as he trailed her across the wide front lawn of Clearwater Crossing High School. A warm fall sun shone down on them, heating up the Missouri Ozarks. "You know what a piece of junk it is."

"You could have let us come pick you up."

"I already told you, Leah! I was covered in grease by the time I called. Besides, I knew it was going to take all day to get that heap running again, and it did. I'm really sorry, but come on. It was only brunch. It's not like I missed seeing you sworn into Congress."

"Lucky for you," Leah muttered. She was willing to believe Miguel's story—he was too self-righteous to be lying—but it was still inexcusable that he'd missed their first date with her parents. If he hadn't been so insistent on driving in the first place, it never would have happened.

"I'll make it up to you. I swear," he promised.

"Hmm," Leah replied, distracted by the sudden realization that there weren't many students around. She pushed through the front doors into a nearly empty main hallway, then nervously checked her watch, thinking they must be late. But no, they still had a couple of minutes. So where was everybody? Hefting her backpack higher on her shoulders, Leah hurried her long strides, and Miguel matched his steps to hers.

When they walked through the open door of Ms. Walker's classroom, though, the sight that met her eyes took Leah completely by surprise—the room was barely one-third full. "Where *is* everyone?" she gasped.

"I'm sure they're all still out in the quad," Ms. Walker said peevishly as Leah and Miguel split up and took their seats. "They're probably thinking that under the circumstances I won't be taking tardies, but they're wrong." She nodded meaningfully toward the open roll book on the lectern in front of her.

"Under what circumstances?" Leah whispered to the girl in the next row. "What's going on?"

"Didn't you see the ambulance?"

"What ambulance? What happened?"

"The cheerleaders were doing a stunt in the quad and Melanie Andrews fell and cracked her head open. They rushed her out of here with sirens and everything. Where were you?"

"Off campus," Leah answered, her voice sounding dead in her buzzing ears. "Is Melanie all right?"

The girl shrugged. "Don't know. No one does."

The tardy bell rang, and Leah turned to face forward in her chair. A few more students straggled in, but Leah barely saw them as her gaze locked with Miguel's. She could tell by his expression that he'd just heard the same bad news.

What should we do? she asked with her eyes.

Miguel shrugged, then glanced toward the open door. *Do you want to leave?* he seemed to reply.

She did, more than anything, but they couldn't exactly get up and walk out in front of Ms. Walker. As if to emphasize the difficulty, the teacher chose that moment to cross the room and close the door. Leah's heart sank as the door thudded into place, sealing off the room like a vault. They'd have to wait.

"Next period," she mouthed to Miguel.

He nodded and turned forward in his seat as Ms. Walker began her lecture.

10

Leah wasn't the rookie biology teacher's biggest fan under the best of circumstances—that afternoon she thought she'd go crazy before Ms. Walker let them out. The lecture dragged on and on, and students trickled in one by one, but the big black-and-white clock at the front of the room seemed to have frozen in place. All Leah could think about was Melanie. Was she okay? Was she in pain? Was anybody with her? A hundred questions raced through Leah's brain, any one of them more interesting than what caused some fruit flies to have curly wings while others had straight ones, the topic Ms. Walker was currently mangling. When the dismissal bell finally rang, Leah was the first person out of her seat.

"Are we going to the hospital?" she asked, meeting Miguel at the door.

His car keys were already in his hand.

"I guess I'd better call my mom," Jenna said, looking around the dejected group.

No one said anything. The other members of Eight Prime were all lost in their separate thoughts and worries for Melanie. Miguel and Leah had shown up an hour after the rest of them, and together they had pulled some of the hospital waiting room chairs over to a sofa against the wall to make an area where they could talk more privately. It was almost dinnertime now, though, and they still hadn't heard a thing. "Back in a minute," Jenna added quietly, heading for a bank of pay phones.

At the phones, Jenna fished some change out of her backpack, dropped it into the slot, and dialed her home phone number. It had barely rung before someone snatched it up.

"Hello?" a girl's voice answered eagerly.

Jenna choked back a groan. Her younger sister Maggie was the last person she wanted to talk to. "Maggie, it's me. Let me talk to Mom, okay?"

"Where are you?" Maggie asked nosily.

Jenna had vowed to be nicer to her sister, but she still found the question annoying. "I'm on the phone. Now go get Mom."

Maggie huffed and dropped the receiver on something hard. "Mom!" she bellowed.

A moment later, Mrs. Conrad picked up. "Hello?"

"Mom? It's Jenna. Listen, Melanie Andrews fell and hit her head at school today. She's in the hospital, and we're all here with her. I'm going to be late for dinner."

"Jenna, that's terrible! Is she all right?"

"I don't know." Suddenly Jenna felt exhausted. "They won't tell us anything, and they won't let us see her, either."

"Then why don't you come home, dear?" Mrs. Conrad urged. "Come home and have some dinner. You can drive my car back to the hospital later if you want. I'll go with you."

12

"Really?" Dinner was the last thing on Jenna's mind, but it would be nice to change her clothes, get rid of her backpack, and sit on something comfortable for an hour. They weren't letting her see Melanie anyway.

"Okay, I think I will. I'll have to get a ride home with someone, though, so I'm not sure when I'll be there."

"Do you want me to come get you?"

"No, Mom," Jenna said, not wanting to interrupt her mother's dinner preparations. "I think Jesse will give me a ride."

"Jesse? Where's Peter?"

"He's here, but his car's at the high school. He rode to the hospital in the ambulance. It's a long story."

"Well, I want to hear all about it. Get here as soon as you can, okay?"

"Okay." Jenna hung up the phone, wishing she were already there. If there was anything she could have done for Melanie, she would have done it gladly. Even just sitting at Melanie's bedside, holding her hand, would have made her feel as if she were doing *something*. But sitting around waiting, not knowing, was wearing her out. She wanted to see her family—happy and healthy and sitting around the dining room table together.

When Jenna got back to the lobby, the other members of Eight Prime were already on their feet.

"They just told us to go home," Peter said. "Melanie hasn't woken up, and even if she does she won't be allowed any visitors tonight."

"Why not?" Jenna protested.

Peter shook his head. "I don't know. They gave us a number we can call tomorrow to see if there's been any change in her condition."

Jenna sighed. Eight Prime had suffered through one crisis already—the death of their classmate Kurt Englbehrt—and it was horrible to think they might be facing another. She glanced at Peter, taking comfort in the thought of riding home next to her friend. But before she could join him and Jesse, Miguel touched her sleeve.

"Do you want me to drive you home, Jenna?" he offered. "Peter told me where you live, and it's not that far from Leah's. I'm dropping her off too."

Jenna bit her lip. She was sure Leah and Miguel had been off somewhere together at lunchtime and that was why they'd missed the accident. There was no way she could ride in a car with them and pretend not to know they were secretly seeing each other . . . not after liking Miguel for so long.

"How are *you* getting home?" she asked Peter abruptly, looking for some way out.

"Jesse's taking me, Nicole, and Ben. We're going to drop her off, then swing by the high school to get my car."

"Oh." Jenna looked back at Miguel, who was still

waiting for her answer. "Okay. Thanks," she murmured unhappily.

The group broke up and Jenna trailed Miguel and Leah out to his car in the far, dark reaches of the parking lot. She couldn't help reflecting that this was her first and possibly only ride in Miguel's old car, any more than she could help wishing it was happening differently. Without Leah, for one thing, who insisted that Jenna take the front seat. Jenna finally relented, sinking reluctantly into the cracked vinyl. No one spoke as Miguel drove out of the parking lot and headed toward Jenna's house. The silence in the car was openly uneasy.

They're afraid I'm going to ask them where they were at lunchtime, Jenna thought bitterly. *Like I want to know!* No way. If she couldn't ignore their couple status, at least she could spare herself the details.

When Miguel stopped at the curb in front of her house, Jenna rushed to get out of the car. "Thanks," she said before she pushed the passenger door shut, purposely stranding Leah in the backseat. "I'll see you two at school tomorrow," she added through the window.

They waved and Jenna hurried up the walkway to her front door, glad to finally be away from them. As much as she liked them separately, she didn't think she'd ever get used to the idea of Leah and Miguel together. It still hurt too much.

15

Jenna's mother met her at the door. "Are you okay, dear? How's Melanie?" Mrs. Conrad's eyes were worried as she reached to put a protective arm around her daughter and draw her into the house.

Jenna tried to tell her, but instead dissolved into tired tears. "I'm fine," she said at last, undone by her mother's sympathy. "Melanie's still unconscious. They're not going to let us see her tonight."

Her mother pulled her closer and rubbed her back. "We'll all be praying for her. You know that."

Jenna nodded mutely.

"I held dinner for you. Why don't you go upstairs and take a few minutes to get ready? We'll eat when you come back down."

Jenna nodded again, gratitude swelling the lump in her throat. With seven people living at home, meals at the Conrads' didn't get held up without a good reason. Jenna knew that postponing dinner was her family's way of showing they cared, that they wanted to help her however they could.

"I'll hurry," she promised, heading for the stairs and the bedroom she shared with Maggie. She rushed up and across the landing to her open doorway, bracing herself for the visual jolt of the ugly posters Maggie had plastered all over her side.

But they were gone! Jenna froze in amazement. Even more shocking, Maggie's side of the room was completely clean. Maggie sat on a neatly made twin bed, an apologetic expression on her face.

"I took down the posters," she said.

"I see that," Jenna managed. Plain white walls had never looked so wonderful. "Why?"

Maggie shrugged. "I was going to do it anyway. But Mom told me about Melanie, so I figured I might as well do it now. I'm sorry, Jenna. I hope she's all right."

"You did this to make me feel better?" Jenna was stunned. "Maggie! Thank you."

"Yeah, well, don't let it go to your head," Maggie mumbled, her freckled cheeks reddening. "I just . . . I'm sorry, all right? About Melanie. And, well . . . you know. About what I said in front of Peter. I promise not to tell anyone else about your crush on Miguel."

Jenna sat heavily on her own bed, unable to take it all in. "Why?"

"Because I don't want to fight with you anymore. Can't we just be friends again?"

Jenna shook her head disbelievingly. That was almost the exact same speech she'd planned to give Maggie, once things had settled down. "I don't want to fight with you, either. And I'm sorry too—especially about getting you grounded and making you miss the Fall Fantasy."

Maggie winced at the allusion to her lost dance, and Jenna belatedly wondered if maybe she shouldn't have mentioned it. "I mean it, Maggie. I'd give anything to be able to go back and do things over. I wish you could have gone."

"You do?"

"I really do. And to prove it, I'll make you a promise: Your underwear's safe with me from now on." Maggie's habit of discarding her bra and panties on the floor had finally prompted Jenna to hang them out the window, which had started the sisters' war in the first place.

Maggie smiled crookedly. "So are we friends, or what?"

"Friends," Jenna agreed. "Come on. We'd better get down to dinner now, before everybody starves."

"Mom said that after dinner me and Allison can make some cookies for you to take to Melanie," Maggie informed her as they started down the stairs.

The mention of Melanie filled Jenna with renewed anxiety. "Maybe you ought to wait," she told her sister. "It's a nice idea, but I don't know when they're going to let me see her."

Or even if, she added silently.

Two

When the first chinks opened in Melanie's night, light streamed in as if someone had punched holes through a bank of storm clouds. Shafts of white burst through the leaden gray. Melanie pushed back from the unwelcome brilliance—back into the warm, enveloping darkness—but the insistent light pursued her.

No, she thought. *No, don't.* She was happy where she was. At peace where she was. She didn't want to leave.

But the darkness in her fuddled brain kept melting. Her storm clouds were breaking up everywhere now, carried away on a cold morning breeze. Their tattered edges drifted across her vision, evaporating like a dream. A dream . . .

Suddenly she realized she must be asleep. And the last thing on Earth she wanted—the *very* last—was to wake up. She held on, held her breath, imagined that she could stop time.

It was hopeless. Even as Melanie willed the clouds back together, they fled, leaving her exposed in the unkind light—an unwilling traveler, back from the dead.

Tears slipped down her cheeks as she opened her eyes, blinking at the strangeness of her surroundings. She was in a small room, much smaller than her bedroom at home, but the details were out of focus. She tried to lift her head . . . found she couldn't. Everything swam around her, and her stomach rose toward her throat with the suddenness of nausea.

Then a woman appeared at her bedside. A beautiful blonde, with long loose hair that brushed the blankets as she bent forward. She was smiling, an expression of incredible love on her face. A jolt of recognition made Melanie's heart race.

"Mom?" she whispered, her voice a dry rasp. "Mom, is that you?"

The woman's smile grew. She stretched out a hand, as if to smooth Melanie's hair. Melanie reached to intercept it, her eager fingers closing over the wrist. For a moment there was a sense of pressure, a whisper of contact. Then Melanie's hand sank through the flesh that wasn't there, balling up on itself, empty. The image lingered behind, shimmering in the heavy air.

"Mom," Melanie whispered longingly.

The vision tilted its head slightly, then slowly faded away.

"No," Melanie whimpered, more tears sliding off her face. *"Please."*

And then a strange thing happened. Melanie thought she felt a hand—a smooth, cool hand stroking her hot forehead. Just a brush, the lightest touch, and it was gone.

The sensation filled her with hope. Hope broke over her like a wave. And then the will to live flooded her again . . . demanding, insistent, irresistible. She opened her eyes wide and gasped—gasped deeply for the first sweet breath that would welcome her back to the world.

"Melanie? Mel, are you okay?" Her father's anxious face loomed into her vision, filling the void her mother's had left.

"Nurse! *Nurse!*" he shouted. "Call the doctor."

Melanie stared uncomprehendingly, ready for him to fade out too. But her father stayed solid while the room behind him cleared into focus.

I'm in the hospital, Melanie realized. In a rush, she remembered the fall from the spirit pyramid and became aware of a dull, throbbing ache at the back of her skull. *I must have knocked myself unconscious.*

A door behind her father opened, and a woman in white bounded through it.

"What's happened?" she demanded, hurrying toward the bed. But when her eyes met Melanie's, she smiled. "Oh, excellent. I'll page Dr. Levenstein."

21

The nurse withdrew from the room, and Melanie's father squeezed her hand tightly. "Melanie," he whispered, gazing down into her eyes. He looked exhausted, and his hands shook uncontrollably. "Melanie, can you hear me?"

"Of course."

His red-rimmed eyes widened, then filled with tears. "Oh, thank God," he sobbed, burying his shaggy head in her blankets. "Thank God you're all right."

Melanie had never heard her father thank God before. It sounded so strange, but she couldn't concentrate. . . .

She closed her eyes, holding his hand tightly as fresh tears seeped through her lashes. The clouds, the darkness, the incredible feeling of safety, were already receding in her memory.

She was alive.

"I don't know why you even bother to meet me for lunch anymore, since you only stay five minutes," Nicole complained to Courtney Bell. "What do you and Jeff do that's so fascinating, anyway?"

Her best friend grinned wickedly from her place on their favorite quadside bench. "I *know* you don't want me to answer that."

"Oh, get out of town," said Nicole, annoyed. Courtney was always hinting around about things Nicole was positive weren't happening—it seemed

22

to give her some kind of thrill. "I barely see you anymore. I can't believe you weren't here yesterday."

"Could you give it a rest?" Courtney asked impatiently, rolling her eyes. "It's not like I missed seeing Melanie crack her head open on purpose. That's probably the most exciting thing that'll happen all year."

"Courtney!" Nicole said reproachfully. The news that Melanie was going to be all right had swept through school first thing that morning, rendering Courtney's remark excusable. Even so, Nicole didn't think it was very nice.

"Oh, please," Courtney returned, unrepentant. "Like you're her best friend. It's how you *treat* a person that counts, Nicole, and I'm a lot nicer to her than you are."

Nicole ground her teeth. She'd have loved to make a scathing comeback, but unfortunately Courtney was right. The irony was that under other circumstances Nicole would have looked up to Melanie even more than Courtney did. After all, Melanie was a cheerleader. Not to mention gorgeous, popular, wealthy, and talented. In other words, she had everything Nicole wanted for herself. *Everything.* Including Jesse Jones. And that was where Nicole drew the line.

"You *are* still going to the U.S. Girls contest with me, right? You're not going to bail on that, I hope." The modeling contest was less than two weeks away now, and any thought of Jesse inevitably reminded Nicole how badly she wanted to win it. That would make him sorry he'd rejected her!

"I said I would," Courtney returned testily. "Well, this has been a ton of fun," she added, tossing her half-eaten lunch into the trash can, "but I've got to go."

Nicole watched as her friend took off across the quad without a backward glance. *If Courtney's throwing food away, she must really be smitten,* she thought, not at all sure how she felt about that. Courtney was headed for the main building, her red hair bright against the crisp fall sky. With a stab of regret, Nicole realized she already missed her.

And now what am I going to do? she thought, feeling suddenly conspicuous, sitting on a bench all by herself. *I can't stay here. I look like a reject.* She was about to move when she caught sight of Peter and Jenna walking directly toward her.

"Hi!" she called brightly as they approached. "You just missed Courtney—she left five seconds ago."

Jenna smiled and took a seat beside Nicole. "That's okay. We were looking for you."

"Oh, right." Nicole nodded. "I just thought . . ." Why did she always feel as if she had to explain *everything*—even the things nobody cared about? "Right. What's up?"

"We're going to the hospital to visit Melanie after school today," said Peter. "Do you want to come?" He stood while Jenna sat, his tall, thin form blocking Nicole's view of the crowd behind him.

"Uh, yeah. Okay." Nicole wasn't thrilled at the idea of making a fuss over Melanie, but she didn't exactly wish her harm, either. Besides, it would look bad if she said no. "What time are we leaving?"

"Right after sixth period," Jenna told her. "We'll meet in the student parking lot."

"All right."

"Good. See you then." Jenna stood to leave.

"Hey, wait! Where are you going?" Nicole asked quickly. "Why don't you hang out awhile?"

"We still have to find Ben," Peter said. "I'm sure he'll want to come with us. You can help us look, if you want."

Nicole could barely keep the sour expression off her face at the thought of spending her lunch break searching for nerdy Ben. The only thing more socially damaging than being seen sitting by herself would have to be being seen doing *anything* with Ben. "No thanks," she said. "I, uh, I'm waiting for someone."

"Okay. See you in the parking lot," Jenna said, and she and Peter took off.

Nicole was stuffing her untouched lunch into her backpack, planning to go hide in the library, when a tall shadow fell across her bench.

"Hey, Nicole. Where are you going?" asked Jesse.

Nicole looked up into his blue eyes and felt her heart turn over the way it always did—the traitor in her chest seemed incapable of remembering how much she hated Jesse now. She wouldn't give him the time of day. Not even though he was alone, for once. And she was alone. . . .

"Well?" he prompted.

"What? Oh, uh, nowhere," she stammered, flustered.

His smile was confident. "Can I sit down?"

"Sure. Of course." Her pulse hammered as she scooted over to make room on the bench, clumsily pushing her open backpack right off the end. She heard it hit the ground and turned to retrieve it, blood rushing to her cheeks.

Be cool! she pleaded with herself. *Or at least don't do anything* more *embarrassing.* This was the first interest Jesse had shown in her since he'd kissed her at that football party and then blown her off. Nicole wasn't sure what was going on, but she definitely didn't want to ruin it.

She turned around with her rescued pack to see Jesse settled onto the other end of the bench. He leaned back, surveying her coolly. "So why are you eating by yourself?" he asked. "Where's Courtney?"

"She's with Jeff—that's this guy she's seeing now. I was just on my way to the library, actually." *There.*

That didn't sound too desperate, Nicole congratulated herself.

"Oh. Well, I don't want to keep you. You'd better get going."

"No! Uh, I mean, um, I don't really *have* to go to the library. I just, uh . . . thought I would. You know, maybe check out a book or something." She knew she was stammering like a fool, and the amused smile on Jesse's face confirmed it.

"Are you going to the hospital after school?" he asked casually, lacing his fingers behind his head and stretching. "Did Peter and Jenna already ask you?"

So that was it—he'd come to talk about Melanie. How could she have thought anything else?

"Yes, I'm going." *Although why you care, I can't imagine.* "Are you?"

"I don't know. I don't think so."

Nicole almost fell off the bench. "What? Why not?"

"I was worried about her yesterday, when she first fell," Jesse said with a shrug. "But now that I know she's okay, I don't see any reason to go."

"But I thought you were so in love with her!" Nicole blurted, then bit her lip. Had she actually just said that?

Jesse winced. "Hardly. We're just friends. We were, anyway."

"Were?"

"We had a fight. Right before she fell." He

27

shrugged again, and Nicole could tell he was trying to act like he didn't care, but his face had clouded over. His eyes avoided hers.

"A fight about what?" she asked breathlessly.

"Just, well . . . we had a little argument Friday night. It was nothing, really. But yesterday, when I tried to apologize, she jumped all over me and told me to leave her alone."

"You're kidding!" Nicole gasped. "I can't believe it."

"It wasn't too nice, that's for sure. I was pretty mad. But then, when I found out she'd fallen, I felt horrible. Like maybe I'd caused it somehow."

"You! You weren't even there!"

"I know. But I'd just finished talking to her a couple of minutes before. . . ."

"It wasn't your fault, Jesse."

"You don't think so?"

"Of course not."

He nodded uncertainly. "Well, thanks. But either way, I don't think Melanie wants to see me."

"Don't be silly," said Nicole, unable to imagine anyone not wanting to see Jesse. "It wasn't your fault, and if you come to the hospital with us, I'm sure Melanie will tell you the same thing."

"I guess." Jesse hunched forward on the bench. "The truth is, I don't really want to see her, either. I know it sounds pretty bad, since she's in the hospital and everything, but I could use a good, long break from Melanie Andrews."

Couldn't we all! thought Nicole.

But somehow she managed not to say that. Instead she gave Jesse her most sympathetic look. "I know how you must feel, but you shouldn't be so hard on yourself. Come to the hospital with us this afternoon and get it over with. *Then* take a break if you want to."

Jesse pulled a face. "I'm going to feel like a fool."

Then suddenly he sat up straighter. "Hey, would you want to ride with me, Nicole? If we all go, we'll have to take two cars anyway. You and I could meet everyone there—and if things get embarrassing, we'll just leave."

"Well . . . sure," said Nicole, stunned. "All right."

Jesse smiled and rose from the bench. "See you after school, then. Later."

"Later," Nicole echoed as he walked off to join some Wildcats by the cafeteria.

She watched motionless from the bench, afraid even to move for fear of waking herself out of the best dream she'd had all year. Jesse and Melanie had had a fight, and now Jesse was turning to her. What an opportunity! Nicole wasn't naive enough to believe he was over Melanie—it was pretty clear he wasn't—but it sure sounded as if Melanie was over him. Not only that, but hadn't he just said he didn't want to see her for a while?

29

And a while is all I need, Nicole thought, wishing there were some way she could go home and change clothes before she met Jesse in the parking lot. *If I can get a few days alone with him, I know I can make him like me.*

For the first time since that horrible Monday he'd dumped her, Nicole let herself remember Jesse's kisses. Her eyes dropped closed at the recollection, and her breathing came faster. To feel Jesse's arms around her again . . . Jesse's mouth on hers . . .

Her eyes flew open abruptly. *You have got to play this cool. Be smart this time, Nicole!*

Somehow—she still didn't understand how—she'd gotten a second shot at this guy. And this time she intended to hit the target.

There was scuffling outside in the hallway; then Melanie's father opened her hospital room door a crack and peered through. "Some of your friends are here to see you, Mel. Do you want me to let them in?"

Her dad had stayed beside her all through the night while she'd slept. He'd left for a while earlier that day, but only long enough to shower, shave, and put on some decent clothes. When he'd come back, he'd brought Melanie the things she'd asked for from home: a thick chenille bathrobe, books, her makeup case, and a hairbrush. To her surprise, he'd also added some items of his own: a new plastic cooler full of fancy bottled waters, a pile of magazines, a box of chocolates, and a big bouquet of stunning pink roses. He'd thought of everything, and tears had brimmed in Melanie's eyes at the unexpected reminder of the way he'd used to be. She suspected he must have had a couple of drinks at home to steady those shaking hands, but at least he wasn't drunk.

Now, still holding the door half-closed, he waited for her answer. "If you don't feel well enough . . . ," he said worriedly, clearly on the verge of sending whoever it was away.

"No, let them in," Melanie croaked. She struggled to sit more upright in the bed. Her head was still throbbing, and she knew she must look terrible, but she felt better than she had that morning. Besides, she was eager to talk to someone who had actually seen her accident and to find out what was being said about it at school. She reached for the bottle of water next to her bed, wetting her throat as the members of Eight Prime filed into the room, led proudly by her father.

"Two of you girls take the chairs, and the other can sit on the bed," Mr. Andrews directed, pulling the chairs up to Melanie's bedside. There were traces of the old executive in his manner as he herded her friends about the tiny room. "You guys will have to stand, I'm afraid. Things are pretty tight in here."

"That's okay," said Peter. He stood, smiling at Melanie, with a small bouquet of flowers in one hand. Ben and Miguel stood on either side of him, and Jesse skulked behind them, his eyes glued to the floor. Melanie shared his discomfort as the recollection of the last time they'd spoken to each other came rushing back. Her cheeks grew hot at the memory of the vicious things she'd said, and for a moment she wished she'd been a little less nasty.

Jenna and Nicole dropped into the offered chairs, and Leah lowered herself carefully onto the foot of her bed. "Does it hurt to have me sit here?" Leah asked worriedly.

Melanie tried to smile but ended up wincing. "Everything hurts. You're the least of my problems."

Peter stepped forward with the flowers. "These are for you," he said, handing her the mixed bouquet. "From all of us."

"Thanks." Melanie held the flowers under her nose, but breathing in to smell them made her head start pounding again.

"Let me go find a vase for those," her father said quickly. He took the bouquet and left the room.

"So how are you?" Jenna asked immediately, patting Melanie's arm through the blanket. "We've all been so worried about you!"

Melanie tried to shrug. "I'm all right. I just split

the skin on the back of my head and bruised things pretty good. They stitched me up while I was still out of it, so I didn't even feel that part. I guess they had to shave part of my head to do it, though." She made a face, imagining a big bald spot on the back of her head. "My dad says it's barely noticeable, but I haven't felt brave enough to look yet."

"I'll look!" Ben offered, rushing forward in the cramped quarters. As he did, he caught a foot in the legs of Nicole's chair and lost his balance. He flailed at the empty air in front of him, on a collision course with Melanie's bed.

"Ben!" Nicole cried.

Leah jumped up to grab him, but it was too late. With an impact that made Melanie gasp, Ben fell onto her bed, planting his face in the blankets somewhere around her knees.

"Ben!" Before anyone else could react, Jesse pulled Ben backward off the bed by his belt, yanking him roughly to his feet and giving him a wedgie at the same time.

Ben's cheeks were flaming as he wriggled his pants back into position. "Sorry, Melanie," he whispered. "Oops."

"Way to go, genius," Jesse muttered under his breath.

Ben turned even redder.

"That's okay. You didn't hurt me," Melanie lied. There was something about the wounded puppy-

33

dog face Ben made whenever he messed up that always made her want to forgive him.

"I was only trying to help," he reminded them all. "I was going to check Melanie's bald spot for her."

Peter chuckled, but Nicole flashed Ben an incredulous look. "If *she* doesn't want to see it, she definitely doesn't want *you* to. Figure it out, Ben. Geez."

At that moment Mr. Andrews walked back in with Eight Prime's flowers in a vase he'd borrowed from the nurses. "We'll put these right here," he said, placing it on Melanie's bedside tray.

"Dad, these are the friends I made at Kurt Englbehrt's carnival," she told him, praying he wouldn't do his usual drinker's amnesia thing and ask, "What carnival?"

Instead of the blank stare Melanie had feared, though, Mr. Andrews nodded knowingly around the room. "That was a good thing you all tried to do. Tragic, the way it came out."

His voice suddenly lost strength, and Melanie knew he was thinking of another tragic car wreck.

"This is Jenna Conrad and Nicole Brewster," she said quickly, to change the subject. "That's Leah." Leah was still on her feet, thanks to Hurricane Ben. "And Jesse Jones, Miguel del Rios, and Peter Altmann. Oh, and Ben." Everyone smiled at her father, but Mr. Andrews seemed distracted.

"Peter Altmann?" he repeated, turning to face Peter. "You're the one who rode with my daughter in the ambulance?"

Peter nodded. "Yes, sir. That was me."

"You did?" Melanie exclaimed. "I don't remember that!"

"Do you remember riding in the ambulance?" Peter asked, surprised.

"Well . . . no," Melanie admitted.

"The principal told me how you refused to leave her," Mr. Andrews said to Peter. "I appreciate that. You're a good friend."

"It was nothing," Peter said self-consciously. "Any of us would have done the same. I was just the only one who could get through the crowd."

"I don't think it's nothing," Mr. Andrews said gratefully. He turned to the others. "When Melanie feels better, you'll all have to come over to the house. We'll grill up some burgers and have a pool party or something."

"It's getting kind of late in the year for a pool party," Melanie protested, but her father only grinned.

"So we'll crank up the heater. If I have to, I'll have one of those big white wedding tents put over the whole deck."

"Cool!" Ben exclaimed.

Melanie wasn't sure what was more frightening: the idea of clumsy Ben by a body of water, or Ben's

35

body *by* the water—in a bathing suit. The thought made her smile despite the pain in her head. "Thanks, Dad. That'll be fun."

The other echoed agreement, and Mr. Andrews beamed, obviously pleased his suggestion had been so well received. Melanie felt an unexpected rush of pride.

It felt great to have her old dad back. She only wondered how long he would stay.

"This is ridiculous," Leah muttered, rolling over in her double bed. She'd lost more sleep since she'd met Miguel del Rios than in the rest of her life put together. "Why does he have to be so *mysterious* all the time?"

The missed brunch had been forgotten for a while in Leah's concern for Melanie, but now that she knew her friend was okay, Leah couldn't get her mind off the subject. Not that she wanted to discuss it with Miguel again. She'd already heard the mechanical breakdown story so many times she could recite it by heart. No, what she wanted to know was whether or not the story was true—that, and why Miguel was always busy on Saturday morning.

Maybe I ought to drop by his house this weekend and find out, she thought, then groaned—she didn't even know where he lived. Not exactly where he lived, anyway. He'd said his house was downtown, but when she'd asked for the address, he'd gotten

36

all weird and evasive on her. *Make that more weird and evasive,* Leah corrected herself. *What is he trying to hide?*

She rolled onto her other side, her restless mind spinning nowhere, like the wheels of an overturned car. *This is going to drive me crazy.*

It wasn't Leah's way to sit by and let things happen to her—she was a take-charge person by nature. And every brain cell she had was screaming to take charge now.

Maybe I ought to follow him home. I could drive Mom's car to school, then tail him home without letting him see me. Leah kicked the idea around a little. It seemed extremely take-charge.

Not to mention extremely dishonest.

Still, it wasn't exactly honest of Miguel to keep her in the dark this way. *Besides, if he isn't doing anything wrong, then he has nothing to fear.*

I'll do it, Leah decided.

She did wish her plan were a little less sneaky, a little less underhanded, but it couldn't be helped.

After all, a girl has to sleep at night, doesn't she?

Three

"Oh yeah," Nicole breathed happily. She'd lost another half-pound! She stepped smiling off the bathroom scale and walked into her bedroom, shutting the door to keep her thirteen-year-old sister, Heather, from barging in from her side of the bathroom.

Now what should I wear? Nicole mused, staring into her closet. Picking out the perfect outfit was even more important that morning than usual. After all, Melanie wasn't going to be at school that day . . . and Jesse was. Nicole hummed as she reached for a denim jumper with flowers embroidered at the neck. Things were looking up.

Not that I'm glad Melanie hit her head, Nicole thought quickly. But, after all, Melanie was going to be fine, and Nicole hadn't made her fall. What harm could there be in taking advantage of whatever good things came from the accident? Jesse's obvious loneliness, for instance.

Nicole crossed to her dresser and picked out a T-shirt to pair with the jumper. October in Missouri was usually one of the nicest months of the year, and the weather so far was living up to expectations. The days were warm and mostly clear, while the nights were crisp and cool. Nicole matched her white shirt with scrunchy white socks.

Wait until Jesse finds out I'm modeling for U.S. Girls, she thought as she pulled the T-shirt over her head, ignoring the fact that competing in a regional model search wasn't exactly the same as walking a Paris runway. Everyone had to get discovered somewhere, didn't they? And if she won the Missouri portion of the clothing chain's contest, the next step would be Hollywood and the national finals! After that, she'd be a model for real.

She had filled out her entry blank the night before, laboriously printing every bit of the requested information as neatly as she could. Even now the sealed, addressed envelope lay perfectly centered on her otherwise empty desktop. She drew in a deep, excited breath at the thought of dropping it into the mailbox on her way to school.

It hadn't been a slam dunk getting permission, that was for sure, but somehow she'd managed. Still high on her success with Jesse the afternoon before, Nicole had worked up the nerve to broach the subject to her parents over dinner. Her father had been dead against it. Looks aren't important, he'd said, and beauty contests are demeaning. Then he'd found out the contest was in St. Louis and he'd really put his foot down.

Luckily, Nicole's mother had taken her side, or that would have been the end of it. "Now, Jimmy," she'd said, turning those shocking blue eyes on him. "Modeling isn't the same thing as a pageant."

Mr. Brewster had raised a skeptical eyebrow. "Is it a bunch of girls getting graded on their looks or am I wrong? I don't see the difference."

"The *difference*," Mrs. Brewster had explained, with just a hint of irritation in her voice, "is that modeling is a career. Besides, I think it will be good for Nicole to take more of an interest in her appearance."

Her mother had eventually worn her father down, and Nicole had spent the rest of the meal wondering whether Mrs. Brewster had any idea how much of an interest she took in her appearance already. Could she really be that blind? And if not, what was she trying to say? That Nicole's interest wasn't paying off?

Nicole sighed now as she tied the laces of her sneakers. She hoped it hadn't been a backhanded way of saying she wasn't very pretty. *No one* was very pretty compared to her mother.

But at least she'd gotten out of taking that pest Heather. The second her father had caved in and said Nicole could enter the contest, Heather had started angling to go along. The little pain in the butt didn't want to enter, of course—she was way too impressed with her own depth for something as shallow as modeling—but she did want to make Nicole ferry her and one of her obnoxious friends to the Skyline Mall. Apparently she wasn't too deep for shopping.

"*Mom!*" Nicole had appealed. "I'm going to be too busy to keep an eye on Heather. Besides, there won't be room in the car."

Thankfully, Mrs. Brewster had decided she didn't want Heather running loose in St. Louis with nobody to watch her. It had been a close call, but Nicole had triumphed. She hoped she'd do as well in the contest.

Finished dressing, Nicole picked up the envelope containing her entry blank. *Please, please, please let me win*, she thought, dropping the precious document into her backpack. Then she shouldered the pack and trotted down the stairs, eager to get to school and pick up where she'd left off with Jesse.

The day before had been a dream: spending lunchtime with him, riding to the hospital in that totally cool car, being dropped off on her doorstep . . . Under the circumstances, even kissing up to Melanie hadn't been that bad. In fact, it was surprising how easy it was to stomach the girl when she looked like death warmed over and had a shaved spot somewhere in that previously perfect blond hair. Nicole couldn't suppress a smile as she reached

41

for the front doorknob. *I can hardly wait to get a good look at that!*

"Could I just get in the closet for one second?" Jenna asked. Both sliding doors were pushed to her side, closing it off.

"In a minute," Maggie mumbled, a glazed, zombie-like expression on her face. She stood gazing into her side of the closet as if it were a crystal ball.

"You've been standing there *five* minutes," Jenna said, trying her best to keep calm. "Just let me get in my side a *second*. I already know what I'm going to wear."

"Huh?" Maggie turned to face her sister. Her tightly wound auburn curls stuck out wildly in all directions, and her skin still held the pallor of sleep beneath its layer of freckles. "Not a morning person" was the nicest thing anyone could say of Maggie at that hour, and, as usual, she was right in Jenna's way.

"Just a second," Jenna repeated, shoving the closet doors over to Maggie's side.

Maggie's expression clouded. Then she shrugged. "Fine. I'll get my stuff out of the dresser."

No! Not the dresser! Jenna thought as her sister shuffled over to the tall, old-fashioned dresser they shared—three drawers each. Why hadn't she thought to get her underwear out while Maggie was fooling around in the closet? Quickly Jenna yanked a shirt and some favorite pants off their hangers, then grabbed a pair of shoes.

Maggie was down on her haunches, staring into the bottom dresser drawer. Jenna walked over and opened the top drawer anyway, rooting around above her sister's head.

"Hey!" Maggie complained, sounding more awake. "You're blocking my light."

"Sorry. I'll just be a second."

"That's what you said at the closet. How come you have to be wherever I go?"

"Because you're *everywhere!*" Jenna exploded. Then, hearing the angry edge in her voice, she forced herself to take a deep breath.

"I'm just trying to get ready for school," she added in a conciliatory tone. She was determined to get along with her sister from now on—no matter how much work it was. "We have to try to stay out of each other's way."

Maggie sighed and opened the next drawer from the bottom, intent on finding who-knew-what. Jenna opened the second drawer down for socks. She had barely pushed the drawer closed again when Maggie stood up unexpectedly. The top of her curly head cracked Jenna under the chin with an impact that slammed her teeth together.

"Maggie!" she yelped, clutching her jaw and staggering backward.

Maggie rubbed at her injured scalp, her eyes squeezed tightly shut. "You weren't supposed to be there," she moaned.

"Where was I supposed to be, then?"

"I don't know. Your chin's *sharp*, Jenna."

Jenna dropped onto her bed, still cradling her jaw, and Maggie sat across from her on her own unmade bed. The two of them stared helplessly at each other, tears of pain glimmering in their eyes.

"If Caitlin would grow up and move out like she's supposed to, we'd both have our own rooms," Jenna said bitterly, unable to fight her frustration any longer. "I mean, look at us—we're wedged in here like sardines! No wonder we fight all the time."

Maggie rubbed her skull tenderly. "You're right," she said slowly. "I wonder why Caitlin doesn't move out."

"I don't *care* why anymore. I just want her to do it. I mean, I love her and everything, but we'd see her just as often if she got a job and stopped mooching off Mom and Dad. She's holding everyone back."

"It would be nice to have my own room . . . ," Maggie mused, as if she'd never given the matter much thought.

"Are you kidding? It would be great! You could put Clue posters on *every* wall if you wanted to— and on the floor and ceiling, too." Clue was Maggie's favorite band.

44

Maggie made a face. "Those ugly things?"

"Then why—" Jenna shut her mouth abruptly. She knew why. "Think about it, Maggie," she said instead. "Our own rooms! What I wouldn't give . . ."

"You hate rooming with me that much?"

"It's not that. It's just . . . well . . . we're getting older, that's all. Wouldn't you like to have a little privacy? Wouldn't it be nice to get something out of the closet without having to wait for me to get out of the way first? Or how about inviting a friend up to *your* room for once, and having it all to yourselves?"

"That would be pretty cool," Maggie agreed, a wistful half-smile on her lips. "But there's no point thinking about it. There's not a spare room until Caitlin moves out."

"Exactly! That's my whole point."

Maggie finally took her hands off her head and scratched at one bare foot. "Caitlin'll move out when she wants to, I guess. There's no way to hurry that up."

Jenna leaned forward intently. "Isn't there? I'm not so sure."

Leah spotted Jenna and Peter eating at an outdoor table by the cafeteria and hurried to join them, her long legs carrying her swiftly through the quad.

"Hey, you two," she said, sliding into a seat next to Jenna on the built-in plastic bench. "I just talked

45

to Principal Kelly about the pumpkin sale. He said we could do it this Friday."

"Friday!" Jenna protested. "But today's Wednesday and we don't even have the pumpkins yet!"

Leah cringed, though she'd expected that type of reaction. "I know. I *told* him that Friday wasn't good for us, but I guess it's good for him. He said there's other stuff happening later in the month, and he can't let Eight Prime conflict with on-campus organizations."

"We're an on-campus organization!"

"Not an official one."

"This is horrible," Jenna moaned. "Melanie won't even be back at school by then. Maybe we ought to forget the whole thing and think of something else."

"We could still have the sale at your church," Leah pointed out, feeling guilty for not asking the principal sooner.

"I don't see why we shouldn't still have them both," Peter ventured, breaking into the conversation. "Maybe we aren't going to do as well here as we wanted to, but we'll still sell some."

"Do you think you can get the pumpkins in time?" Leah asked hopefully. "Because Principal Kelly did say he'd mention the sale in his homeroom announcement for the next two days. And he'll let us hang posters in the halls. I'm up for trying if you are."

"I'm pretty sure I can get them tomorrow if I arrange it this afternoon," Peter replied. "I'll make some calls as soon as I get home from school."

"I can make some signs," Jenna offered. "You know, maybe this isn't such a big deal after all. We have the money to buy them with all ready."

"Sure," said Peter. "And even without Melanie, we still have seven people to sell them. It'll be fine."

"I'll make some signs too," Leah said, relieved they'd decided to go ahead with the plan. She'd have hated thinking she'd let the group down. "Do you need any help picking up the pumpkins?"

Peter shrugged. "Probably not, but I'll give you a call if I do. The most important thing you can do right now is start spreading the word."

"Right." Leah nodded. "I think I'll go look for Miguel. If I catch him in time, he can tell the water polo team about the sale at practice this afternoon. People need to know to bring money on Friday."

"Good idea," said Peter, rising to his feet. "Come on, Jenna. Let's go find Jesse and see if he can tell the football team."

Jenna stuffed an empty sandwich bag from her lunch into a paper sack and tossed it into the trash. "Could you look for Nicole, too?" she asked Leah. "We'll try to find Ben."

"Sure. No problem."

Jenna and Peter walked off toward the gym,

while Leah turned and hurried back across the quad toward the bench Nicole always ate on. As she closed the short distance, Leah saw Nicole sitting right where she'd expected. It was the person she was sitting *next* to who caught Leah by surprise. Courtney's red head was nowhere to be seen. Instead, Nicole was eating with Jesse, a ridiculously oversized smile on her satisfied face.

Well, well, Leah thought. *This is pretty interesting.* Nicole was obviously in heaven, and a smile crept onto Leah's lips too. *I wonder if those two are an item.*

She dismissed the thought the next second. *Two people can't even eat lunch together before you've got them married with children,* she reproached herself. *They're just friends.*

Yeah. Like you and Miguel, a rebellious little voice snickered back.

"Surprise!" the CCHS cheerleaders shouted, bursting into Melanie's room. The entire squad had come to visit her Wednesday after school.

"How do you feel?" Angela Maldonado asked, tying a green-and-gold balloon bouquet to the foot of Melanie's bed. "You *look* good," she added, sitting down.

Melanie knew that wasn't true, but she smiled anyway. As usual, Angela's heart was in the right place. And Melanie *did* look better than she had the day before, when Eight Prime had come to visit. Tanya Jeffries had secretly called ahead to warn her, giving Melanie time to put on some makeup. She still had a bandage on the back of her head, but a nurse had helped her check out her stitches with a mirror that morning, and her father had told her the truth—when she was allowed to wash her hair and comb it normally, the shaved spot would be all but invisible.

"This is a heck of a way to get out of a few days of classes," Tanya teased, dropping into the chair closest to the bed. Vanessa Winters took the other chair, and Lou Anne Simmons, Sue Tilford, Tiffany Barrett, and Cindy White crowded in behind her. "You just about gave us all a heart attack. Come to think of it, I'm actually kind of surprised Ms. Carson isn't in here with you." Ms. Carson was the cheerleaders' part-time advisor.

"She telephoned earlier, and sent me some flowers." Melanie pointed to a bouquet near the window. "She sounded pretty upset."

There was an abrupt, awkward silence. The girls looked down and shifted their weight self-consciously, and Melanie knew she'd struck a nerve.

"In fact, she said she didn't even know we were doing that spirit rally on Monday," Melanie went on. "And that she'd never have allowed us to do that stunt on concrete if she had."

All eyes turned to Vanessa.

"I don't have time to tell her every little thing!"

their captain said defensively. "I only thought of it Sunday night, and I had to call all of you. I had no idea she'd care."

"I doubt she would have if she hadn't gotten in trouble," said Tiffany. "If Melanie hadn't fallen, everything would have been fine."

"Well, excuse me!" Melanie retorted. Her head still throbbed with the slightest motion, and she could have happily skipped sparring with Tiffany. She wasn't even sure why the older girl had shown up. It had to be for appearances' sake—the same reason Lou Anne and Sue and probably Vanessa were there too, Melanie realized suddenly. She was glad her father had gone home to rest—she was much happier to have had him meet Eight Prime. Maybe everything in that group wasn't perfect either, but at least they weren't phony.

"Don't be silly," Tanya said, shooting Tiffany an annoyed look. "We're just happy you're okay, Melanie."

"Yes. Of course," echoed Angela.

"But we aren't allowed to do the new stunt anymore," Lou Anne told her. "Principal Kelly said no way. We can still do the spirit pyramid, but not with the flip."

"*And* we're getting a new advisor," Cindy put in. "Someone who'll actually come to our practices and plan our events and everything."

"Who?" Melanie asked, looking to Vanessa.

Vanessa's face was expressionless, but her voice was hard. "I don't know."

Ooh, she's not happy about this at all, Melanie thought. The corners of her mouth twitched, and she fought to suppress a smile. *I think Queen Vanessa sees an end to her reign.*

"Whoever it is is bound to be an improvement, though," Tanya said. "They could grab someone off the street who'd do better than Ms. Carson."

"Maybe we'll even get to go to cheerleading camp next summer," Angela added excitedly.

"Don't get your hopes up," Vanessa said caustically, and Melanie couldn't hold back her smile any longer. If they *did* go, Vanessa wouldn't be with them. She, Cindy, Sue, and—best of all—Tiffany were seniors. They'd be graduating.

The cheerleaders stayed another ten minutes; then the nurse came in and told them they had to leave. Melanie was just nodding off when a blond head peeked through her doorway.

"Peter!" she said, struggling to sit up. "I didn't think you guys would be coming again today."

"Sorry. It's only me."

Melanie felt her heart lift unexpectedly. "That's even better," she said, surprised by how happy the sight of him made her.

"Really?" Peter took the chair Tanya had recently vacated, a shy grin on his face. "I didn't know I was that exciting."

Actually, Melanie hadn't known so either, but right then she couldn't think of anyone she'd rather see. She liked the rest of Eight Prime, but the group was nothing without Peter. He was the heart and soul of their circle, the reason it existed. It was impossible to even imagine them together without Peter and his Junior Explorers. Melanie returned his smile, wondering if Jenna knew how lucky she was to have such a great best friend.

"What are you doing here?" she asked.

"I wanted to see how you're feeling. I've been praying for you."

A few weeks before, a statement like that would have made her squirm. Now she only smiled. "I know. I hope it does me some good."

"You're still with us, aren't you?"

"Yeah. And about that—why couldn't you have prayed I'd wake up in Hawaii, or someplace *good*?"

"Very funny." But his smile said he knew she was joking.

"You know, Peter, I've been thinking," she said, suddenly serious. "There's something so weird . . . I don't remember you being with me when I was unconscious, but I think somehow I must have known you were there."

"What makes you say that?"

"I don't know. It's just a feeling I have. I knew somebody was with me."

"Oh. Well, I don't see why your subconscious

couldn't have known. I was talking to you. And holding your hand."

"You were?"

Peter blushed and ducked his head. "Well . . . yeah. I was terrified, Melanie. For a while there, I really thought you were going to . . ." He let the sentence trail off and looked directly at her, making his eyes say it for him.

"Yeah, me too." *I almost* hoped *so,* she nearly added, but she couldn't tell him that. Not Peter.

"When we got to Emergency and they made me go sit in the lobby, I thought I'd go crazy with wor—"

"Wait. You mean you weren't with me the whole time?" Melanie interrupted, startled. She'd been so sure her companion was Peter. . . .

"I *wanted* to be. They just wouldn't let me." Peter shook his head as if throwing off a bad memory. "But, hey, you're all better now. When are they letting you out of here?"

"Tomorrow, I think."

"That's great! So when are you coming back to school?"

"Not right away. Dr. Levenstein says not before next week, and my dad says I can stay out as long as I want to."

He nodded. "You should take your time. I'm afraid I have some bad news, though. We have to hold the pumpkin sale at school this Friday."

"*This* Friday? We said we'd wait till later in the month!"

"I wish we could. Especially now. We all wanted to wait for you to be well. But this Friday is the only day Principal Kelly will let us do it. I made some calls before I came over, and I've got the pumpkins all arranged. I'm picking them up tomorrow after school."

"Are you holding the sale at your church this weekend too?" Melanie hadn't been wild about the church idea, but now she wanted him to say he at least wouldn't do that part without her.

"It would be better, if it's okay with you. Otherwise I have to unload all those pumpkins and find a place to store them."

"Unload them from where?"

"My dad drives a big pickup, and he's going to let me use it for the sale. Once it's loaded, it'll be a lot easier to leave the pumpkins in back until we sell them all."

"Oh." Melanie sank into her pillows a little.

"I'm sorry, Melanie. I wish you could be there."

"Yeah, well. We don't always get what we want in this world."

Peter winked. "Just one more reason to look forward to the next one."

Melanie's head ached, and she was desperately disappointed about missing the sale. Even so, she

54

smiled a little. "You never give up, do you?" she teased.

But after Peter had gone, she thought about what he'd said. Could there really be another world, something after death? Before her accident, she'd have called that type of talk wishful thinking. Now . . . now she wasn't so sure.

She closed her eyes and tried to imagine herself in that blackness again. Had she really been close to dying? If so, why hadn't she been scared?

Because I knew I wasn't in danger, she thought, twisting a fistful of blanket as she struggled to understand. *I mean, I didn't feel like I was.*

It was strange, but she'd have sworn there was someone with her the whole time . . . someone . . .

But if it wasn't Peter, then who?

Four

What a drag, Jesse thought, glancing around the crowded quad on Thursday for someone to eat lunch with. *Every day the exact same thing.*

Of course it didn't help that he'd been playing like crap lately. His last game had been a disaster, and—as if that weren't bad enough—he'd stunk in every practice since. His teammates weren't being very supportive, either. The big joke going around the locker room was that Jesse Jones couldn't catch a cold standing naked in the snow. Hanging out with the Wildcats lately took more courage than sense, but with Melanie out of the picture, who else was he going to hang out with?

Not that Melanie was likely to be speaking to him. She'd seemed calm enough about seeing him at the hospital, but how nasty could she really get with her dad and all of Eight Prime crammed into that closet of a room? He had a feeling she wouldn't be nearly so nice if she ever got him alone.

Jesse's eyes wandered to a group of his fellow football players, and glanced away again. He hesitated outside the main building, unable to decide what to do. Then his eyes lit on Nicole and Courtney, sitting on their usual bench. Eating with them was bound to be better for his ego than eating with the Wildcats. He took a few steps in their direction, stopped, and reluctantly changed his mind. He'd spent lunchtime with Nicole the past two days in a row. It was kind of fun to watch her panic when he walked over, but he didn't want to give her the wrong idea. Not again.

Shrugging he turned and walked along the edge of the quad, past the cafeteria. When he got to the access road that ran through the school, he turned again and headed for the student parking lot. What he needed was to get off campus for a while.

What I need is to get out of Sticksville, Missouri—and not just for a while. Jesse imagined climbing into his gleaming red BMW, pointing it west, and driving—all night, all the next day . . . however long it took. Southern California beaches were still sunny in October. He had a credit card. . . .

Jesse yanked his car door open and climbed in, seriously tempted to take off. *It's not like the team would miss me,* he thought, feeling more and more sorry for himself. He pulled onto the road and turned right, no destination in mind.

No one would miss me. Not the team. Not Melanie, that's for sure. I doubt Dad would even notice I was gone, he's so busy with Elsa. The mere thought of his

57

snobby, too-young stepmother brought an unconscious sneer to Jesse's lips. What had his father been thinking when he'd married that gold-digging piece of fluff?

Streets, houses, and finally barns slipped by as Jesse drove farther and farther from school. He glanced at his wristwatch, knowing he'd never get back by the bell, not caring. "What are they going to do to me?" he muttered, unable to think of a single thing that could make him feel any worse.

And then the road turned narrow and winding, and Jesse finally knew where he was going. A short drive later he rolled into the unpaved parking lot at the edge of the lake, his tires spewing dust that was snatched away on a crisp fall breeze. The same breeze troubled the water, whipping the surface of the lake into hard-looking ripples against a sharp-edged sky. Jesse watched from behind his windshield, not sure why he was there. He switched on the radio, then settled back into his seat, letting his mind wander.

He'd come to swim at the lake with some of the football players twice the past summer. All the local kids seemed to think the place was great, but the thick, dark mud that oozed disgustingly between his toes and those unidentifiable hunks of green glop floating in the water made Jesse long for the ocean. After the second trip, he'd begged off in favor of the sparkling clean pool at the country club.

He hadn't completely lost interest in the lake, though—not after he'd learned it was the school makeout spot. He'd brought a couple of girls there to park during those hot summer nights: Vanessa Winters and a tennis pro from his club named Katie. He wouldn't have minded seeing Katie again, but the age difference had turned out to be a problem for her. She'd been afraid of losing her job, or worse, and Jesse hadn't much cared either way. One night with Vanessa had been enough, though. After the beer had worn off, he couldn't even remember what he'd been thinking.

Jesse sighed. He didn't know what it was with him, but it had always been the same. He liked girls—they just couldn't hold his attention. Not the dozens he'd fooled around with back home, not Katie, not Vanessa, and certainly not Nicole. Whatever it was that was supposed to click just never fell into place for him. He'd get interested in a girl, pursue her for a while, take her out once or twice, and then totally lose interest. *More* than lose interest, actually—never want to see her again. He realized it was a pattern; he just didn't know how to break it.

And then Melanie Andrews had caught his eye, and for a while he'd thought that everything could change. There was something about Melanie that drove him nearly crazy. Even when she looked right at him, even when she pasted on that fake cheering-squad smile and flirted as if he were the only guy in town, Jesse was certain she barely even noticed him.

How could she? It always felt as if she were barely even there, as if she had a split personality or something. Jesse had only ever seen the girl on the surface, but he was sure there was another one down deeper—there had to be. And somehow he'd managed to convince himself that she was the one girl who could change his life.

He shifted in his leather seat and turned off the radio in one impatient swipe. "You're so full of it," he muttered. "If you ever got Melanie, you'd dump her, too. It's who you are. It's what you do."

"Here we are," Mr. Andrews announced, pushing Melanie's bedroom door open with his foot. "One cheese omelet, as promised."

Melanie watched apprehensively as he carried the tray to her bed and set it shakily on the edge. When he released it without incident, they both breathed a sigh of relief. All week long her father had been doing his best to stay sober, but the effort was taking a toll. Although he was dressing, shaving, and combing his hair again, his complexion seemed almost gray, and his hands shook so badly that Melanie could barely stand to look at them.

"Well, go ahead. Eat up." Mr. Andrews sat in a chair next to the bed and nodded toward the tray. Somewhere in the Andrewses' huge kitchen he'd found a covered silver dish, the kind hotels used for room service. Or maybe he'd gone out and bought it—Melanie wasn't sure. Pulling the tray onto her lap, she lifted the cover and looked underneath.

"Ta-da!" exclaimed her dad. And then he started to laugh.

Melanie looked from what could only be called scrambled eggs—and scrambled was a kind description—to her father in amazement. She didn't care about her lunch. She just couldn't believe how strange it was to hear him laugh again.

"I tried," he said, pointing to the plate, still chuckling. "I think you must need some special kind of pan for omelets."

"Yeah. And probably someone who knows how to use it," Melanie couldn't resist teasing.

"Well." He waved one arm dismissively. "Eggs. Cheese. It's all going to look the same in your stomach."

"Thanks for the mental picture. I'm *really* hungry now."

"You have to eat something, though. Okay Mel?" he said, serious again. "If you want, I'll go out and get you something else, but you have to eat."

"Don't worry, Dad. This is fine." She picked up her fork and took a bite. "Actually, it's pretty good."

"Okay. Now I know you're lying." But the worry eased in his blue eyes. "You know, Mel," he said suddenly, "I don't know what I would have done if

61

anything had happened to you. I couldn't stand it. Not after losing your mother . . . not you, too."

"Nothing happened to me, Dad," she said, not wanting to go where the conversation was leading. "I'm fine."

He shook his head. "You didn't see yourself lying on that stretcher. When they first brought me in, I took one look and my heart almost stopped. I swear it did. All I could think was that if you died I didn't want to live."

"Dad—"

"No, let me finish." His cheeks were flushed, and his eyes betrayed his emotion. "I haven't been a very good father to you lately, Melanie."

She opened her mouth but found she had no reply. His words were a total shock.

"I'm sorry. I've only been seeing what I've lost. I—I'd like to say I'll change, but . . . I *do* love you, Mel. I hope you know how much."

"Then . . . then *prove* it." Melanie dropped her fork and pushed the tray away. "Be my dad again. Be the way you were."

His expression became more guarded. "I'll always be your dad. But I'm not the same man anymore. I don't even want to be. I'm sorry, Melanie. I'm sorry your mom died."

"Mom's accident wasn't your fault, Dad. I don't want you to apologize, I want you to do the things you *can* do."

But Mr. Andrews suddenly lurched to his feet. "I—I'm sorry," he stammered, hurrying out of her room.

Melanie heard his bedroom door shut a moment later. And as badly as she wanted to believe otherwise, she knew he was digging through his dresser or his closet or wherever he kept the booze.

Great, I drove him to drink, she thought, feeling a lump grow in her throat. She'd always known his sobriety wouldn't last—couldn't last—but for a while there she'd lost her head. For a while she had almost hoped. Her father was actually talking about things that mattered again. Hadn't he just said he loved her? And she'd believed him.

She still believed him.

Leah ducked quickly behind the dashboard, flattening herself in her mother's white hatchback. Miguel was walking along the edge of the student parking lot, his dark hair wet from water polo practice. She'd caught only the briefest glimpse before she'd hidden. Now, her heart pounding with a mixture of nerves and curiosity, she slowly raised her head to peek through the windshield.

She had intentionally parked as far from Miguel's old sedan as possible. There was almost no chance he'd see her, especially since he didn't know what her mother's car looked like, but Leah wasn't taking any chances. Her mind was made up to tail him home, and having him spot her now wouldn't be good for her plan.

Miguel's car coughed to life, and Leah started her engine under cover of the noise. Miguel pulled out of his space and drove to the main exit. Leah let her car roll quietly backward into the aisle. Not until Miguel turned left onto the road did Leah sit up straight and put the car in gear, hurriedly driving after him. Miguel's car was already disappearing down the street when she reached the exit, and she rapidly turned to follow it. She gave the car a burst of gas, gaining ground, then reconsidered and let herself drift back. She knew he was going downtown—there was no point sitting on his bumper.

Miguel drove slowly until traffic thickened and the roads widened. They were getting close to downtown. Leah's pulse quickened, and she gripped the steering wheel more tightly, ready to act instantly when Miguel turned down a side street toward home.

But Miguel didn't turn. Instead he drove straight through the center of town, right into the commercial district.

"Where is he going?" Leah whispered. There weren't many residential areas downtown, and they had just passed the turnoffs for the ones she knew of.

"Oh, no!" she groaned a moment later as a horrible thought occurred to her. What if Miguel wasn't going straight home? She could be following him anywhere.

"Brilliant," she muttered, disgusted with this unexpected turn of events.

They were almost all the way through town now. Leah wondered whether she ought to cut her losses and turn back before Miguel saw her, but it killed her to abandon her plan when she'd already come so far. Besides, it hadn't been easy getting her mother to lend her the car. Who knew when she'd get it again? *I'll stay with him*, she decided.

The streets they were cruising now were ones Leah had rarely seen. The back side of town was old and run down. There wasn't anything of interest there, just the railroad tracks, some rotting, rickety wooden houses, and a few rusty old warehouses.

Where's he going? She was starting to feel a little nervous. *What's he doing here?*

The streets had become potholed, and the sidewalks and curbs were cracked and heaved by the roots of enormous old trees. A smell of mildew and rotten wood pervaded the air. Leah dropped farther behind as Miguel led the way past a row of abandoned brick storefronts with their windows boarded up. She was tempted to turn back, but she knew she wouldn't rest until she found out what Miguel was up to in this sad, decayed old neighborhood.

And that was when he pulled to the curb and parked.

Acting on reflex, Leah cranked the steering wheel hard to the right, turning down a gravel road. She immediately regretted her decision. The road was deeply rutted, and the car bounced wildly, forcing her to slow down.

As she drove, she noticed a group of tough-looking older guys watching her from the driveway of a decrepit house, like sharks eyeing a tired swimmer. One lot over, a house had burned down, leaving a charred, broken slab. Leah's heart hammered as she pulled into its overgrown driveway and turned around. Then, headed the right way again, she drove gratefully back toward the paved road, sweat prickling at the nape of her neck. When she reached the pavement, she turned right, in the direction she'd last seen Miguel.

To her horror, Miguel was still in plain view, barely fifty yards away, fooling around in his car. Leah cringed, expecting him to turn and lock eyes with her any second. He had parked just past the edge of the ramshackle houses, where the local housing authority provided small, government-subsidized cottages for the elderly and the poor.

You idiot! she berated herself, looking desperately for an escape route. *Why didn't you go in the other direction?*

She'd been a fool to follow him into a place she barely knew—she was sure to get caught now. With nowhere to turn, she put her foot on the brake and stopped at the side of the road, praying he wouldn't look her way.

But Miguel never saw her. Instead, he got out of his car and locked the door, then stepped over the curb and onto the grassy front yard of the nearest cottage. Leah watched curiously, wondering what he was up to. Then, before her astonished eyes, he slipped a key into the front door lock, let himself into the little brick house, and pulled the door closed behind him.

He lives *there!* The realization hit her like a bolt. *Of course!*

That was why Miguel wouldn't give her his address, why he didn't want to bring her home to meet his mother. It had nothing to do with being embarrassed by *her*. He didn't want her to know he lived in public housing.

"Of course," Leah whispered, already over the shock.

It was so like Miguel to worry about something that didn't matter at all. So he was poor. She'd already known that, and she couldn't care less. True, she hadn't realized he was *this* poor, but now she felt as if she should have. When Miguel's father was alive and working, Leah supposed that the del Rioses had been alright. But now, with the loss of their major breadwinner on top of the fact that they hadn't any health insurance, well . . . their finances could only have gotten worse.

Leah pulled away from the curb and made a U-turn in the street.

This is good, she thought as she headed for home. *This is better. I'll tell him tomorrow that I don't care where he lives, that things like that don't matter to me. Then he can stop sneaking around and—*

Oh. Oh, great.

How could she tell him she didn't care where he lived when she wasn't supposed to know? She couldn't exactly tell him she'd been spying on him—he'd think she didn't trust him.

You didn't *trust him,* she reminded herself.

Yeah, but I don't want him *to know that.*

And then Leah remembered something else. Following him home had only been the first step in her plan. The real goal had been to find out what kept him so busy on Saturday mornings.

"Great," she said out loud.

It seemed her spying days weren't over.

"Caitlin?" Jenna called, knocking on the third-floor door after dinner Thursday evening. "Can I come in?"

She pushed into her sister's room without waiting for an answer and found Caitlin reading a novel in the overstuffed chair by the window, her legs dangling over one of the padded arms. The sky outside was dark, but a floor lamp next to the chair spilled a pool of light over Caitlin and her book, dissipating into a cozy glow in the corners of the room. Caitlin's big double bed was neatly made beneath its flowered comforter, her desk and bookshelves were arranged with artistic exactitude, and in the middle of the floor, in that precious open space, was a braided rug constructed of years of the Conrad girls' discarded old jeans. The faded denim made a warm blue splash on the varnished wood floor, stretching to Caitlin's slippered feet like the waters of a miniature lake. Jenna stood just inside the door, so mesmerized she'd temporarily forgotten why she'd come. Compared to the hecticness of the rest of the house, her sister's enormous attic bedroom seemed like Heaven come to Earth.

"Hi, Jenna," Caitlin said, putting down her book and twisting around to sit in the chair properly. "Is something the matter?"

"Uh, no. Why do you say that?" Jenna walked in and took the rolling wooden chair by Caitlin's built-in desk.

Caitlin smiled. "You don't come up to visit very often."

Jenna felt a little jab of guilt. She wasn't exactly on a social call this time. "Well . . . I . . . homework. You know."

Caitlin glanced longingly at her immaculate desk. "You'll probably think I'm crazy, but I kind of miss having homework. I see all you guys studying

69

away, even Sarah, and it feels weird not to be working too."

Jenna smiled. She couldn't have asked for a more perfect opening. "It must be pretty boring for you, hanging around here all day . . . nothing to do. I don't know how you stand it."

"Oh, it's not that bad. I help Mom with things, and I read a lot. I don't miss school, only the homework."

No. She'd be happy to skip school, Jenna thought. Caitlin had always been too shy to make any real friends there. She'd hung around their older sister, Mary Beth, as much as she could, but Mary Beth had graduated and gone off to college two years before, leaving Caitlin behind and alone.

"Caitlin, why don't you get a job? I mean, I'm not criticizing or anything. I just want to understand. It doesn't make any sense to me that you hang around here when we're so crowded and you could be out on your own. Think of it—if you moved out, you could do whatever you want."

Caitlin dropped her eyes. "I guess there isn't anything I want to do that bad," she said, her voice so low that Jenna could barely hear. "I'm not like you, Jenna. I'm not like any of you."

"Oh, come on. You say that like you're from a different planet. I know you're shy, but people *do* get over that, Caitlin. For Pete's sake, you're eighteen! When Mary Beth was eighteen, she couldn't wait to get out of here and go do her thing."

"I'm *definitely* not Mary Beth." Caitlin's voice was quavering now. Her eyes were on the floor.

"Look, I'm sorry, Cat," said Jenna, reverting to her sister's childhood nickname. "I didn't come up here to upset you. It's just . . . well, Maggie and I are so crowded. And by the time you were my age, Mary Beth had moved out and you had this nice big room to yourself. I was really hoping . . . I mean, I thought . . . Oh, never mind."

"You thought I'd move out and that you'd get this room for two years too, the same way I did."

"Exactly!"

"I'm sorry, Jenna." Caitlin pushed up from the chair and stood at the dark window, looking out where there was nothing to see. "I've been thinking about this a lot, especially lately. And I knew . . . I knew I ought to let you have this room, but I couldn't stand to give it up. I've been selfish. But since I don't have a job, I don't have any real money. There's no way I can move out. Even if I found work, it would take months to save enough."

"Oh." Jenna's heart sank as she realized anew how remote her chances were of getting her own bedroom. She had hoped that dropping a few well-chosen hints might make Caitlin realize it was time to get a life—and let everyone else have one too—but the situation seemed hopeless. Before Caitlin could get

71

an apartment, she'd have to get a job. Then she'd have to save her money. Then she'd have to *find* an apartment. And that was even assuming she was motivated, which apparently she wasn't.

"Like I said," Caitlin repeated, "I've been thinking about this a lot. Every day, in fact. I can't move out." She hesitated, then took a deep, shuddering breath and straightened her shoulders determinedly. "What I *will* do, though, is move in with Sarah. That ought to make things a little more fair."

"Huh?"

Caitlin finally faced her. "It's your turn to have this room, Jenna. I'll move in with Sarah, and Allison can move in with Maggie.

"I—I—you would *do* that?" Jenna stammered, overwhelmed.

"Sure. Why not?"

Jenna shook her head. "I don't know. It just never occurred to me." *And I thought* everything *had occurred to me!* How could she have missed such a simple, such an obvious, solution?

"Do you want to do it on Saturday?"

"Huh? Oh. You bet!" She still couldn't believe it was happening. It was as if a stranger had walked up and handed her the keys to his castle. And it was going to happen so *soon!* Saturday was only two days away. "Thanks, Caitlin. You're the best! Listen, I'm going to go tell the others, okay?"

Caitlin nodded, and Jenna practically flew out of

her room, eager to spread the good news. Sarah wasn't going to care one way or the other; Allison would be ecstatic to move in with Maggie, who was one year older instead of two years younger; and Maggie . . . well . . .

Maggie might not be totally thrilled, she admitted. After all, Jenna had kind of hinted that they could both get their own rooms.

But it's not my fault that didn't work out! She reassured herself as she hurried down the stairs. *Besides, Maggie ought to like being the older girl for a change. She and Allison will have more fun together than she and I do.*

Jenna hugged herself excitedly and did a fancy leap off the bottom stair. She couldn't wait for Saturday!

Five

"Well, good luck with your little pumpkin thing," Courtney told Nicole as the two of them came out of the main building. "I'd hang out and help you, but . . ." Her smile said it all. She was going off campus with Jeff. Again.

"Aren't you at least going to buy a pumpkin?" Nicole asked worriedly. "And what about Jeff? We have about a million of them."

The members of Eight Prime—minus Melanie— had arrived at school early that morning to watch Peter drive his father's truck into the farthest corner of the quad, its tailgate facing back toward the center. Principal Kelly had said they could bring the truck onto the grounds to avoid having to carry the pumpkins in by hand. They'd unloaded a bunch, arranging them into groups on the pavement so that people could see them better. They'd just finished when the first students started wandering past on their way to morning classes.

"Come back at lunch," Peter had called to everyone who walked by. "It's for a good cause."

Ben had taken up the cry, hawking pumpkins as if he were selling tickets to the circus. "Come one, come all! We've got the best darn pumpkins in town."

Nicole winced to even remember it. She hoped this sale wasn't going to make them all laughingstocks. She'd have felt a whole lot better if Melanie was going to be there. With Melanie Andrews out in front of the group, what could people really say?

"I'll catch you after school," Courtney promised. "Where are you guys going to be? By the student parking lot?"

"I guess," Nicole answered grimly, feeling as if she were about to face a firing squad.

"Oh, buck up. Joining the God Squad was *your* bright idea." Courtney always referred to Jenna and Peter that way. Being completely without faith herself, she found theirs immensely irritating.

"Thanks for reminding me."

But Courtney was already gone, off to find Jeff. Nicole hesitated on the edge of the quad, then took a deep breath and crossed to meet her friends. Leah, Ben, Miguel, Peter, and Jenna were already there, busy trying to sell pumpkins. To Nicole's surprise, however, so were Angela Maldonado and Tanya Jeffries, dressed in their cheerleading uniforms.

"Hi, Nicole!" Jenna greeted her enthusiastically as she reached the makeshift pumpkin patch.

75

"Look who Melanie sent to help us! Do you know Angela and Tanya?"

Nicole fidgeted, a nervous smile on her face. Of course she knew them—she knew all the cheerleaders. What she *didn't* know was whether or not she should admit it. What if they didn't remember her? Then she'd look like an idiot. On the other hand, if she pretended she didn't know them, they might think she was clueless, or totally stuck-up.

Tanya put her out of her misery. "Sure. Hi, Nicole."

"Hi!" Angela echoed. "Isn't this fun?"

"Yeah . . . um, fun," Nicole replied, barely able to believe her good luck. Here was her chance to make friends with two of the girls who would be selecting next year's cheering squad! Not to mention the fact that just having the cheerleaders around made selling pumpkins a lot more cool. Nicole heaved a sigh of relief. Maybe this wasn't going to be so bad after all.

"Hey, Nicole!" Ben bellowed suddenly from right beside her. Nicole jumped, startled, then grimaced. She wasn't sure she was ever going to get used to the way Ben always sneaked up on her.

"How much is this pumpkin?" He held out one of the larger ones as if he actually expected her to know.

Nicole's eyes skipped irritably from the pumpkin to his face, then widened with horror—the oblivious little geek was actually wearing an orange base-ball cap stuffed and painted to look like the upper half of a pumpkin, complete with a hokey green stem and a leaf on top.

"I don't know. What pile was it in? No, never mind," Nicole added hastily before Ben could reply. "Go ask Peter." She actually shoved him in the back to hurry him on his way.

"He's, uh, well, he's . . . ," Nicole tried to explain to the cheerleaders as Ben trotted off.

"Ben," Tanya finished for her. "Melanie told us all about him."

Nicole smiled, weak with relief that they weren't going to hold Ben against her. *She couldn't possibly have told you enough*, she thought.

A moment later, though, it occurred to her that Melanie might have told them all about *her*, too. "I guess we'd better get busy," she murmured un-comfortably, not even wanting to imagine what Melanie might have said.

The three of them spread out to answer ques-tions and help prospective customers find exactly the right pumpkins. Nicole liked the feel of the heavy gourds in her hands—some rough, some smooth. She handled them carefully, doing her best to sell them to the milling crowd, but there seemed to be more lookers than buyers.

"Where's Jesse?" she asked Leah huffily after

several precious minutes had ticked away and she still hadn't made a sale. "Why isn't he helping us?"

"He's trying to get a bunch of the Wildcats to come over. He should be here any second."

"Hey, *Nicole!*" It was Ben again, another pumpkin in his hands and that ridiculous hat still on his head.

Nicole winced. "What?"

"Look at this one! It's got a butt crack!" He laughed as if delighted by his own cleverness. "Look, you guys," he added excitedly, flashing it at Tanya and Angela.

Tanya smiled, but Angela looked completely shocked.

"Ben!" Nicole squealed, embarrassed. "Get that out of here! I'm sure!"

"I'm going to show it to Miguel," he said, spinning around. But as he did, he lost his grip on the offensive vegetable. It flew out of his hands and hit the pavement in front of Angela's feet, exploding into a hail of goopy orange pieces that rained down on her pristine white Nikes.

"Ben!" cried Nicole.

As usual, Ben looked positively mortified. His cheeks turned pink and his eyes squeezed shut behind the thick lenses of his glasses. "Sorry," he murmured.

He was *always* sorry—so why did he never learn?

"That's okay," Angela said kindly. "It'll wash off."

"No, it's going to stain," Nicole moaned.

Angela looked less thrilled. "Well, if it does, I can always polish over it."

"Wow, Angela. I feel really bad about this." Ben stared down at her messy shoes, then looked up all of a sudden, an inspired expression on his face. "Here. Take my hat," he offered, whipping it off his head.

"Ben!" Nicole screeched.

"No, really, Angela," he insisted cluelessly. "I *want* you to have it."

Angela was no doubt searching for some polite way to decline when Jesse burst loudly onto the scene, a group of football players in tow. "Here we are!" he shouted. "Show me the pumpkins!"

Nicole immediately deserted Ben and Angela, hurrying forward to point out the best ones. The guys jostled and joked and fooled around, but she managed to sell them three, and she saw other members of Eight Prime succeed in selling some too.

Then things really picked up. Students who had spent the first half of the period eating lunch were finished now and were wandering over to check things out. People squatted on the pavement to get a better look, while others pawed through the back of the truck. Nicole ended up next to a pile of the smallest, least expensive pumpkins, selling one after another.

Lunchtime slipped away, with people actually shoving money at her during the last few minutes before the bell. Jenna was working a few feet away, and Miguel and Jesse had taken over the big pile next to the cash box, but Nicole couldn't see anyone else—they were all on the other side of the truck. It occurred to her briefly to wonder who Ben was bothering, since he seemed to have given up on her, and she prayed it was Peter or Leah instead of the two cheerleaders.

When the first bell rang, there was still a big crowd swarming around the truck. Nicole sold a few final pumpkins to students anxious to get to class. Within a couple of minutes, though, the quad had emptied. Nicole looked down at the gourds remaining on the concrete, expecting to see the place cleared out after such a flurry. To her surprise, there were lots of pumpkins left. Not only that, but the back of the truck looked practically full.

This is not good, she thought. It had seemed as if they were selling tons, but now she saw that they had barely made a dent. *If we don't do a lot better after school, we're going to have a big problem.*

An unexpected burst of wild laughter from the other side of the truck distracted her. She turned in time to see Angela and Tanya stagger out into the open quad, holding their sides and giggling, Ben right on their heels.

"Did you think that was funny?" he asked eagerly. "I know a million of those."

Nicole could barely believe her ears. Ben was telling jokes now? And those cool girls were *laughing*?

But that wasn't the worst thing—not by a long shot.

Angela was wearing Ben's silly pumpkin hat. It sat at a jaunty angle atop her long dark curls. And the thing was, on her, it actually looked cute.

"That's a good one," Jesse assured a skinny girl inspecting a pumpkin beside him. "You should get it."

The after-school sale was under way. Peter and Jenna had been allowed to leave sixth period early to set up near the student parking lot, and the moment the bell had rung, Jesse and the rest of the group had rushed out to help them.

"I don't know . . ." The girl moved to the next pumpkin and bent to look it over.

As far as Jesse could tell, they were all exactly the same. He fought to control his impatience. And then he had an idea.

"I don't think I've ever seen *you* before," he said smoothly. His unsuspecting victim glanced up, and he flashed her his flirtiest smile. "Did you just transfer in from somewhere?"

81

"No. I, um, I'm a freshman."

"Really? Wow, I never would have guessed that." *Oh man, are you a liar*, he thought with a silent snicker. "What's your name?"

"Ann." She was blushing already, coyly ducking her head. It would have been hilarious if he'd been in a better mood.

"Well, Ann, if you want my advice, you ought to get that one right there." Jesse pointed to one of the larger pumpkins, strictly at random. "That's practically the best of the bunch."

"Do you think so?" she asked, rushing to check it out.

"Oh, definitely. And don't forget what a good cause it's for. All the money helps disadvantaged children."

Ann ran her hand over the warty skin of the pumpkin. "Well, okay."

Moments later Jesse was stuffing her bills into the cash box, waving as she staggered off under the pumpkin's weight.

I've still got it, he congratulated himself. But the thought didn't give him a thrill. Hardly anything did anymore. He hated to admit it, but he missed Melanie. He missed her a lot, in fact. He wondered what she was doing, and whether she was sorry to be skipping the sale.

She must be, he thought. *She sent Tanya and Angela, didn't she?* The cheerleaders had shown up to help again after school. Jesse glanced to where they were working with a crowd of guys around them.

He'd never really noticed before, but Angela was pretty hot. Not only that, but she looked almost ridiculously cute in that stupid pumpkin hat of Ben's. Something about the color really showed off her brown eyes and the glossiness of her dark hair. She had a tiny beauty mark next to her mouth, too. He'd never really noticed before. . . .

A second later, he sighed. *Don't do it, man. Not Angela.* It wasn't as if he didn't have enough trouble already.

He'd stunk in football practice all week, but the day before he'd been so especially pathetic that he'd been afraid even to ask for an afternoon off to help with the sale. All week long Coach Davis had been totally disgusted with him—yelling and screaming and pulling his hair—and Thursday afternoon the coach had shouted himself hoarse. When Jesse had approached him in the locker room, he'd fully expected the coach to jump all over him.

What had happened had actually been worse. "Yeah, good idea," Coach Davis had interrupted before Jesse had even fully begun his explanation about the Junior Explorers and the bus Eight Prime hoped to buy them. "Take an afternoon off. We could *all* use the break."

"How much did we make, Nicole?" Jenna asked.

Nicole shrugged. "I don't know. I don't really feel like counting right now." Her blue eyes shifted to the load of pumpkins remaining in the truck, and Jenna knew what the problem was.

"Don't worry. We'll sell them at church this Sunday," she said reassuringly.

"I hope so."

Jenna hoped so too. They hadn't done nearly as well at school as they'd expected. If only they'd had more time to put up posters and let people know to bring money!

Leah shouldn't have waited so long to talk to Principal Kelly, Jenna thought, glancing at her. Leah had spent most of the sale avoiding Miguel, but Jenna saw the way they looked at each other, and it still felt like a slap in the face every time. *It wasn't Leah's fault*, she told herself hurriedly, determined not to blame her friend for the disappointing sales simply because she was jealous. *Any of us could have asked the principal anytime.*

"Should we pass the cash box?" Peter asked, walking up to them. Eight Prime had passed the money from hand to hand after its two previous events to celebrate its accomplishment.

"I guess," Jenna and Nicole said in unison.

Nicole handed the box listlessly to Jenna, who

handed it to Peter, who passed it off to Jesse. The box made its circuit, but there wasn't the usual sense of victory that day. Everyone seemed depressed, and it didn't feel right without Melanie there to join in.

"Look," Peter said, tucking the cash box under his arm. "I know we didn't do too great today, but we didn't do that badly, either. I think we sold about a hundred."

"That means we have *two* hundred left," said Nicole. "How are we going to get rid of them all?"

"Have a little faith, Nicole. We still have the sale at church this weekend, and if they don't get taken there, we have time to think of something else. Maybe we can sell them in the park."

Nicole didn't look too thrilled, but she didn't say anything more. The rest of the group was silent too. Jenna had noticed before that Peter had that effect on them. Whatever he said, they all just seemed to accept it as if he were in charge.

"Do you need help unloading these pumpkins somewhere, Peter?" Miguel asked.

"Thanks, but I'm just going to back the truck into the garage and leave it there. My dad will drive my car until after the sale on Sunday."

Miguel nodded. "All right, then. Do you need a ride home, Leah?" he asked, turning toward her. "It's on my way."

To Jenna's annoyance, Leah actually pretended

to consider. "Um . . . all right. Thanks," she agreed before the two of them walked away.

The rest of the group broke up quickly, leaving Peter and Jenna with a truck full of pumpkins. The afternoon shadows were growing long, but it was still early enough for them to do something together before dinner. *Maybe after we put the truck away, we can go for a bike ride or—*

"Well, we'd better get going," Peter said. "I'll drop you off on the way so you don't have to walk from my house."

Jenna looked at him blankly. He wanted to take her straight home?

"My dad has the Toyota," he reminded her, "and once I've got this beast in the garage, I don't want to move it again. Besides, I've got a lot of homework."

"All right," Jenna agreed uneasily. She climbed up into the high cab of Mr. Altmann's truck, buckled her seat belt, and attempted to smile as if nothing were wrong. In her heart, though, she knew something was. Ever since Peter had found out about her crush on Miguel, he'd been strangely aloof. Not unfriendly, exactly, just detached somehow. Not there. Jenna knew he was upset she hadn't trusted him with her secret, but she'd assumed he'd get over it in a day or two. Now she was starting to wonder.

I probably should have told him about Miguel, she

admitted to herself as Peter started the engine and ground the cranky old truck into gear. *But he's overreacting. It's not like I withheld life-or-death information.* Jenna shook her head, worn out by her best friend's attitude.

Why does he even care?

Six

L eah killed the engine and glided silently down the tree-shrouded street, feeling slightly ridiculous. It was practically the crack of dawn and she was wearing a hat and sunglasses. Not only that, but she was driving as if she thought she was Jane Bond, sneaking up on Miguel's house from the opposite side of the street and rolling to a stop at the curb about fifty yards away. It wasn't an optimum viewing site, but she was afraid to go any closer. From where she had parked, she could see Miguel's car and his little square of front lawn, and if she leaned way forward she could just glimpse the front of his house.

"This is good. This'll be fine," Leah muttered nervously, tilting her seat back and slouching down until she could barely see over the dashboard. Her eyes firmly on Miguel's tiny yard, she settled in to watch. The great mystery of how Miguel spent his Saturdays was about to be revealed.

Unfortunately she was there much too early. Not only wasn't there any action at the del Rios residence, but nothing was happening on the rest of the street, either. An hour went by, and Leah began wishing she'd slept in. Her long legs were getting cramped, and her tailbone ached. Even worse, the interior of her mother's hatchback was becoming uncomfortably hot, thanks to the low sun shining though the windshield. The rising warmth in conjunction with her half-horizontal position was putting her to sleep. She tried to fight it, but she'd gotten up so early . . . and her eyes were so tired . . .

She was just dropping off when a kid on a bicycle whizzed by her door, catching her totally unaware. The unexpected motion so close to her hiding place shocked Leah into wakefulness. She sat bolt upright in her seat. Then, remembering what she was doing, she threw herself back down. She was still trying to slow her erratically pounding heart when Miguel walked into his yard.

There he is!

She squashed down even lower, wishing she were invisible. Miguel paced his little square of lawn, his eyes on the ground as he walked back and forth. Then he walked toward the house, out of Leah's view. *Now what's he doing?* She lifted her head an inch, straining to see. Minutes later, Miguel reappeared with an old-fashioned hand lawn mower and began pushing it briskly across the grass.

Leah sank back down in her seat until all she

could see was the top of his head. *That isn't exactly the deep dark secret I had in mind*, she thought, disappointed. Actually, she didn't know *what* she'd had in mind anymore, but it definitely wasn't yard work.

I can't believe he made up all those stories just to keep from saying he had to cut the lawn!

She still didn't believe it. There had to be something else. She settled in to wait, determined to know what it was.

When he was done with the mower, Miguel raked up the cuttings. Then he bagged them and swept the sidewalk. With nothing to do but sit and compare, Leah gradually realized that the del Rioses' small yard was the nicest one in sight. The others were reasonably well kept, as if there were some type of routine lawn mowing done for the whole complex, but Miguel's domain was clipped, raked, and swept to perfection.

"Miguel!" a girl's voice called.

Miguel straightened up and looked toward his house.

"Are you almost ready? Mom wants to go to the bank, too."

Miguel nodded. "All right. Just a minute."

The girl's reply was too soft to carry, but Leah did hear the sound of the front door closing. Miguel began gathering up his tools—the mower, the rake, a rusted metal weed claw. Then he went around the side of his house and reappeared without them, going in at the front door.

I should leave—this is my chance, Leah thought. Obviously a trip to the bank wasn't anything she needed to see. *If I do it now, I can be gone before he comes back outside.* But something made her hesitate. She still hadn't learned what she'd come to find out. Maybe he had something else to do after the bank.

Miguel reappeared in a clean polo shirt, his hair freshly combed, followed by a beautiful teenage girl and a woman who could only be his mother. The three of them crossed the newly manicured lawn to Miguel's beat-up old car. Miguel opened the passenger door and helped his sister and mother in. And then he looked up, directly at Leah.

Leah froze, her heart in her throat, her breathing all but suspended. She was scrunched way down in her seat, barely visible, still wearing her sunglasses. *Does he see me?* she thought in a panic, slinking down even lower. *Does he know it's me?*

But Miguel didn't seem to notice her. He walked around his car, dropped into his seat, closed the door, and started the engine.

Leah exhaled, a long, slow sigh of relief, then suddenly realized she was in worse trouble than before. He was going to drive right by her! She threw herself hurriedly facedown across the passenger seat, not daring to move until the rumble of Miguel's engine had receded into nothingness.

"Whew! That was close," she whispered shakily, sitting up.

Then, with a start, she remembered she was supposed to be *following* him. She turned her key in the ignition and made a rapid U-turn in the shady street. Stepping down on the gas, Leah shot off in the direction the del Rioses had gone, praying she hadn't already lost them.

"I don't think I'm cut out for this spy stuff," she grumbled, trying to wriggle some feeling back into her legs as she cruised the empty streets. "I should have read more Nancy Drew."

"Are you moving the beds, too?" Maggie asked. "How are you going to do that without asking Dad to help you?"

"We don't need to move any of the furniture," Jenna replied. "We'll just swap." She had everything all worked out, and she hummed happily as she pulled clothes out of her side of the closet and laid them across her bed.

Downstairs, her mother was practicing piano in the living room, working on a new song to teach the choir. The chords floated soothingly to the second floor. Jenna had always loved listening to her mother play, and for a moment she stopped to wonder if she'd be able to hear the instrument from another floor up. She shrugged. *If not, I can always hear it at church*, she reasoned. It was a small price to pay for a room of her own.

Then another, less easily dismissed thought came to her. *I hope Mom isn't going to freak out when she sees us changing rooms*. Jenna had a sneaking suspicion she should have asked permission first, but she hadn't. On the contrary, she'd instructed the other girls to keep the big news to themselves. She was getting worried now, though. *I guess I could still say something*.

Caitlin poked her head in through the doorway. "I'm on my way to take some things downstairs . . ." She trailed off, looking around at the chaos on Jenna's side of the room. "But I can wait, if you're not ready for Allison."

"No! No, send her up," Jenna said hurriedly. "Tell her most of the closet's empty." The stuff that had come out of it was still spread all over Jenna's bed, but that was a minor detail. "Is it okay if I start taking things up to your room?"

"You mean *your* room, don't you?" Caitlin asked with a faint smile. "Sure. Go ahead."

Jenna paused only a second, then scooped a random armload off the bed, a grin spreading across her face. "Thanks, Cat!"

She edged past her sister and raced up the stairs to the third floor. The door stood open. Bursting excitedly into her new room, Jenna ran to the center, then stopped and stared. Caitlin had already packed everything and set it in boxes near the door. The bedroom was empty, waiting for her. Clear morning light streamed through the open window and gleamed on the polished floor. The closet doors were pushed to one side, exposing a completely empty space twice as big as the one she'd just vacated. The desk was bigger too, and she'd never had her own bookshelves before. And drifting up from downstairs—just barely, just enough—Jenna could still hear the sound of her mother's piano.

It was perfect.

"And it's all mine," Jenna whispered, completely, blissfully happy. "Peace at last."

The music downstairs stopped suddenly, breaking Jenna out of her reverie. She walked to the closet and began hanging up her clothes.

"Jenna!" her mother called. "Jenna, come down here, please."

Uh-oh. Jenna's heart leapt nervously against her rib cage. There was no mistaking that tone of voice. Mrs. Conrad did *not* sound happy.

"Coming!" Jenna tossed her armful of clothes onto the stripped double bed—*her* double bed—and ran, taking the two flights of stairs in record time.

"Did you call—?" she began, rushing into the living room, but the sight that met her eyes there knocked the rest of the thought right out of her head.

Mrs. Conrad had risen from the piano bench. Caitlin and Sarah stood dejectedly to óne side of her, while Maggie and Allison shifted their weight nervously on the other. All five of them were staring right at Jenna.

"Sarah tells me she's moving," Mrs. Conrad said, clearly displeased.

"No! Not *me*, Mom," Sarah corrected. "*Allison*. Allison's going to Maggie's room, Jenna's going to Caitlin's room, and Caitlin's moving down with me!"

"Does that sound about right?" Mrs. Conrad's eyes never left Jenna's.

"Well, um, yeah," Jenna said. "That's the plan. I mean, uh . . . if it's all right with you."

"Don't you think you should have asked me that *before* everyone started moving?"

"Probably." Jenna hung her head. She had come so close . . . *so* close . . .

"Then why didn't you?"

Jenna took a deep, frightened breath, but told her mother the truth. "I was afraid you'd say no. You're so opposed to me having my own room. But this way worked out perfect and everyone was happy and I really wanted to do it and—"

"I'm not *opposed* to you having your own room, Jenna. There just isn't one available."

"But there *is* now."

"And as for everyone being happy, I doubt that applies to Caitlin." Her mother's brows drew into a disapproving frown. "I've told you before, I won't have you badgering her about that room. Caitlin will move out when she's ready, and not a moment before. You have no business asking her to move in with Sarah."

"I didn't!" Jenna cried. "It was *her* idea!"

"That's true," Caitlin put in softly. "I offered."

Mrs. Conrad turned to face her older daughter. "But why, Caitlin? You don't have to do that. Jenna can wait until—"

"No. I want to," Caitlin insisted, stunning them all by interrupting. "It's fair, Mom. Let us do it."

"Well." Their mother was nonplussed. "I don't like it."

"*Please?*" Allison piped up. "I'm tired of sharing with a baby like Sarah. I want to move in with Maggie."

"I'm tired of sharing with you, too." Sarah stuck out her tongue.

Jenna held her breath.

"Are you *sure* Jenna didn't bully you into this?" Mrs. Conrad asked Caitlin.

"No, Mom. It's fine."

"You're eighteen and you're going to be rooming with a ten-year-old."

"I know."

The five girls stared expectantly at their mother.

"Well . . . if it's what you all want . . . ," she said reluctantly.

"Yippee!" Allison shouted, throwing a sweater into the air.

"Yippee" was an understatement. Jenna's chin jerked up. Her eyes widened with disbelief. "Do you mean . . ."

"I still don't like it," Mrs. Conrad added sternly. "But I won't stop you."

Jenna rushed to hug her. "Oh, thanks, Mom! You're the best!"

"You'd better thank your sister," her mom said dryly.

Jenna let go of her mother and spun around to crush the older girl in a hug. "Thanks, Cat! You're the best too." The way she felt right then, she could have hugged Maggie and told her *she* was the best.

"Can we finish moving now?" Allison demanded.

"I guess so." Mrs. Conrad sat down at her piano and began to play again.

The sisters hesitated only seconds, staring at each other with excited expressions, then ran off to resume their move, whooping and giggling as they went. Jenna charged up the first flight of stairs to her old room, grabbed as many clothes as she could carry, then ran up the second flight of stairs to her new room. She was hurriedly hanging them in the closet when Maggie's voice called up from the landing below.

"Jenna! It's Peter!"

Jenna hooked the final hangers over the bar. "Peter's here?" she called back.

"He's on the phone, genius. What do you think?"

Jenna hadn't even heard it ring. She trotted down the stairs and started into her old room.

"Oh, no! You're not using *our* phone," Maggie told her, winking at Allison.

"Yeah, Jenna. Go downstairs." Allison smiled conspiratorially at Maggie, who gave her a slight, approving nod.

Great. Five minutes and she's already poisoned Allison, Jenna thought, but she ran down the stairs to the first floor anyway, hoping she hadn't created a monster by letting those two room together. *Maybe I should have told Caitlin to move in with Maggie instead.*

"Hello?" she gasped when she reached the kitchen telephone. "Peter?"

"What are you doing? Running laps?"

"Practically. I just found out my new room doesn't have a phone. I can't even hear it ring in there. I had to run all the way to the kitchen."

Peter chuckled. "Everything's a trade-off."

"You know, now that I'm thinking about it, I'm pretty sure Mary Beth took the one that used to be up there when she went off to college. I can't believe Caitlin's gone two whole years without a telephone, though. She's never said a thing."

"I guess she doesn't use one very often."

"Apparently not."

Then Jenna remembered it was Saturday. "Hey! What's the deal? Why aren't you at the park with the Junior Explorers?"

"I am. Chris is watching them for a minute. Listen, my dad let me have the Toyota, and I was thinking of going to Melanie's to see how she's doing. Want me to swing by later and pick you up?"

Jenna made a face, not a bit in love with that suggestion. "Can't we do it tomorrow after church? I just started moving my things and I want to get my room set up."

"Tomorrow we have the pumpkin sale, remember? And then I have to do something with the leftover pumpkins, and wash my dad's truck, and get everything back to normal."

"Oh. Right."

"You don't have to come, Jenna. I just thought you might want to."

"I *do* want to. But not right now."

"So . . . no problem. I'll tell Melanie you said hi."

They talked a couple more minutes; then Peter had to go. Jenna hung up, feeling half guilty and half relieved. On any other day, she'd have been happy to visit Melanie, but Peter's timing was horrible. *I'll do it later*, she promised, running out of the kitchen and back up the stairs.

"You can't come in here like that anymore," Maggie protested as Jenna barged into her old room to pick up more of her stuff. "You have to ask if it's okay now."

Jenna raised an eyebrow. "I humored you on the phone thing, all right? Don't push your luck."

"But—"

"Once I finish moving out, I'll never come in here again. How's that?"

"Deal!" Maggie agreed triumphantly. She beamed at Allison as if she'd actually accomplished something, and the two of them dissolved into satisfied giggles on Maggie's bed.

Jenna shook her head and grabbed her guitar case from under her bed, pairing it up with a duffel full of shoes before climbing to the third floor. She was winded by the time she got there. Dropping the duffel, she crossed to her bed and sat down, planning to shove the guitar underneath. But as she bent to do so, it occurred to her that she didn't have to keep the instrument stowed out of sight anymore. There was plenty of space in her new room to put it somewhere better.

She looked around with a critical eye. *I'll lean it in the corner by the window,* she decided. Then, just for kicks, she flipped the case up onto her bed and popped its buckles open, breathing in the familiar smells of guitar and blue velveteen. She hadn't played since that summer, she suddenly realized—not since she'd been a counselor at Peter's two-week camp for the Junior Explorers. And even though her guitar playing wasn't nearly as good as her singing, the kids had loved to have her teach them silly camp songs around the fire at night.

She pulled the guitar out of its case and slipped the shoulder strap over her head, strumming a few chords. Then she began to sing: " 'Ohhhh, they built the ship *Titanic* to sail the ocean blue. . . .' "

"Oops. Sorry, Jenna. Didn't mean to interrupt." Caitlin had come back for more boxes.

"No! Don't worry about it!" Jenna put the guitar hurriedly away. "I was just fooling around. There'll be plenty of time to play later."

Caitlin nodded, grabbed two boxes, and left.

There'll be plenty of time to do lots of things, Jenna realized, standing up and spinning around with excitement. Practice guitar, decorate, read, just sit and think in peace. Maybe she'd even keep a journal now that she was away from Maggie's prying eyes.

"This is going to be the best!" she whispered happily.

"Melanie? There's someone here to see you, sweetie."

Melanie looked up from her lounge chair on the back porch. Her father was coming through the kitchen door, Peter right behind him.

"Peter!" she exclaimed, surprised. The paperback she'd been reading dropped, forgotten, to the concrete. "I didn't know you were coming."

"I should have called first," he apologized. "Is this a bad time?"

"No, of course not." She motioned for him to take a chair beside her in the shade, thanking her lucky stars that her father was dressed and still reasonably sober.

Peter sat, but her father didn't leave. "Are you still okay out here?" he asked uncertainly, walking over to tuck the quilt around her legs. "It's getting pretty cloudy. Maybe you kids should come inside."

"We will in a while," Melanie told him. "I'm fine, Dad."

"Well . . . okay," he said, heading reluctantly into the house. "Call me if you need anything," he added before he closed the door.

"How will he hear you?" Peter asked when Mr. Andrews had gone. "Your house is even bigger than it looks from outside."

Melanie rummaged under her quilt and pulled out a cellular phone.

Peter grinned. "I should have guessed. Here." Leaning forward, he put a tinfoil-wrapped package on her lap. "The cookies are from my mother, and

102

the card is from your buddy Amy. She made it to-day during Junior Explorers."

"That's so sweet!" Melanie pulled a folded square of paper stiff with paint—Amy's card—out from under the yellow ribbon tied around the cookies. "Your mom is so nice. She even put a bow on them."

"I did the bow," Peter admitted, a slight flush creeping into his cheeks. He looked quickly down at his feet so that his hair fell forward, hiding his eyes.

Melanie couldn't believe he was so embarrassed by a little bit of ribbon. The mere idea seemed incredibly cute and old-fashioned.

"Let's see," she teased. "Yellow. If this were roses instead of ribbon, I'd have to say you liked me."

Peter's head jerked up. His eyes looked panicked. "Well . . . I . . ."

"As a *friend*," Melanie explained, laughing. "That's what yellow roses mean—friendship."

"Oh," Peter said relievedly. "Well, I *do* like you as a friend. Of course I do. Read Amy's card."

"*To Melliny*," she read aloud, gazing at its front. "Did you help her with the spelling?"

"Very funny."

The face of the card featured two skirt-wearing stick figures holding hands, the taller one with yellow hair, the shorter one with black. Melanie opened it and read inside:

103

Dear Melliny, I'm sorry you broke yore head.
Dont be sick any more. OK?

Love, Amy

"The kid has a way with words," she joked, not wanting Peter to know she had a lump in her throat the size of a fist.

"She was pretty upset when she found out you'd been in the hospital all week and nobody had told her. She thought Chris and I should have brought the Junior Explorers there to see you."

Melanie's eyes widened as she tried to visualize sixteen rambunctious six- and seven-year-olds and their two counselors crammed into the room she'd had at the hospital.

"It boggles the imagination, doesn't it?" said Peter, reading her mind.

She smiled. "Where's Jenna today?"

"She and her sisters are swapping rooms and she was right in the middle of it when I called her. She says hello, though. She wishes she could have come."

"That's okay." Actually, Melanie was kind of glad that Jenna hadn't made it. There was something she'd been wanting to tell Peter—something she'd never tell anyone else.

"So, how's your head?" Peter asked. "Are you feeling any better?"

Melanie nodded. "I'm sick of being in bed, but

when I walk around I get a headache. I finally convinced my dad to let me lie down out here so I could at least get some fresh air."

"Your dad seems nice. He was really worried about you in the hospital. When you first came in and he passed us in the waiting room, his face was as white as a sheet."

"Yeah." Melanie wasn't about to speculate on other possible causes for his paleness. "He was pretty shook up."

"It must be a big relief to him to have you home again."

"Yeah. Hey, Peter," she said, switching gears. "You know what we talked about at the hospital? About how I thought maybe I knew you were with me, even though I was unconscious?"

Peter nodded.

"Well, it wasn't just in the ambulance."

"What do you mean?"

"It was so weird . . . I don't know how to explain it. It's just that the whole time I was passed out, I felt like somebody was with me, like I wasn't alone anymore. I mean, not that I'm *alone*. But this was different."

"Uh-huh."

She could tell by his smile that he'd already decided she'd had some sort of close encounter with God. That was okay—she'd known he was going to.

"At first I thought it must have been you. I

mean, after I found out about you riding in the ambulance. Then you told me they separated us at the emergency room . . . but there had to be doctors around the whole time. Later, my dad came. So after that I thought it *wasn't* you—that it was a bunch of different people."

"Uh-huh."

Melanie had to avert her eyes to keep from smiling too. "The thing is, that doesn't make sense either. It was one person with me from the moment I blacked out till the moment I woke up. I know it was. I *felt* it."

"But you've already ruled out all the possibilities," Peter said, finishing her thought. "You know there wasn't any one person around the whole time."

"Right."

Their eyes locked. Peter wasn't smiling anymore. "So then who do you think it was?"

"I . . . I don't . . . do you think it could have been my mother?" she asked in a rush. "I mean, I *saw* her, Peter. At my bedside. I opened my eyes and there she was."

"You were dreaming," Peter suggested gently.

"It didn't feel that way." Melanie shook her head. "It didn't feel that way at all."

"You already know who I think it was. Your mother may have been watching, but I don't think she's the one you felt beside you."

"Then why did I see her?"

Peter shook his head. "I don't know. Maybe because you felt the type of love you used to get from her. Is that what it felt like?"

Her heart beat faster as she thought about the question. It *had* felt like love.

"Or maybe it was an angel."

Melanie snickered involuntarily. She was glad Peter was taking her seriously, that at least he believed she'd seen *something*, but an angel?

"I thought angels weren't supposed to look human," she said, straining to remember what little she knew. "Isn't that what it says in the Bible?"

"They can take human form. Perhaps, if one wanted to comfort you, then—"

"Then you think it could have looked like my mother?"

"Maybe. Or maybe you just thought it did. I'm not saying it *was* an angel, Melanie. I'm only saying search your heart. Be open to the possibility. You already know that I think God was with you the whole time. I think you felt his presence. But he could have sent an angel."

"You really believe that, don't you?"

Peter smiled. "You know I do."

"Yeah."

If only she could believe it too. And then she remembered something else Peter had once told her.

107

"You *can* believe, Melanie," he'd said. "You just have to decide that you want to."

"Peter," she said slowly, "you know how you said people can change their minds about God?"

"Yes."

"Do you think that really happens? I mean, *really*?"

"I think it happens every day."

"Why?"

"Because I think he calls people. He calls people and they feel it. Maybe they don't know that's what's happening—or maybe they don't want to believe that's what's happening—but they come just the same."

Melanie was silent a moment, wondering. Was that what was happening to her? It sounded so far-fetched. Yet there was something deep inside her that ached. Something that yearned, and she didn't know why. All she knew was that when she looked at Peter, she saw what she was missing. Calm . . . peace . . . purpose.

"Do you think . . ." She paused, then rushed ahead. "Do you think maybe I could go to your church sometime?"

He looked surprised for only an instant; then a smile lit up his face. "Sure! Do you want me to pick you up tomorrow? I could run you home quick, before the pumpkin sale starts."

"No." She was touched by his eagerness, but she already regretted the unguarded words that had tumbled from her mouth. What could she have been thinking? She already knew she didn't fit in at church.

"Just sometime . . . maybe. I'll let you know."

Seven

Jesse sat in the back pew of Peter's church, feeling conspicuous and out of place. It had been a while since he'd been to services, and he'd never been to this church before. He would have liked to sit quietly and get his bearings before the service began, but Peter had decided to bring a few Junior Explorers along to help with the pumpkin sale. One of the more boisterous kids, Jason, squirmed at Jesse's side, looking stifled and uncomfortable in his navy blue blazer.

"Jason, bud, sit still," Jesse whispered. "You're making me nervous."

"It's hot in here," Jason complained loudly. "When is something going to *happen*?"

Heads swiveled around. Jesse felt himself blushing under the scrutiny.

"Soon," he whispered back.

Just then the choir began filing in. "Look, here comes the choir. See if you can spot Jenna."

"That's easy," Jason returned scornfully, pointing. "She's right there." Jenna was near the front of the line, her long brown hair swinging loose down the back of her white robe.

A hymn was announced, and the choir began to sing. The congregation stood to join in, and Jesse was glad of the chance to let Jason stretch his legs. Jesse took the opportunity to check out the other members of Eight Prime, wondering whether they were having as much trouble keeping their charges quiet as he was. Ben and Leah were on his other side, with a girl called Cheryl between them. Miguel and Peter were farther down, with Lisa and Priscilla, and Chris and Maura had Amy and Elton.

The pastor finally started speaking, and everyone sat down. Jason seemed less distracted now that the service was under way, and Jesse leaned back in the pew, remembering when he was a little boy and had worn blue blazers and fidgeted in church with his family. His *real* family, not the Dr. Frankenstein assortment of mismatched parts he lived with now. Going to church with his stepmother and her spoiled daughter wasn't the same thing at all. How could Jesse believe in answered prayers while sitting next to such hard, bitter evidence of their past ineffectiveness? He hadn't complained a bit when church attendance had ceased after their first few weeks in Missouri.

He remembered when he was little, though. Before the divorce, before his brothers had gone off to college, before Missouri . . . He remembered sitting next to his mother with his oldest brother, Kevin, at his side to keep him in line. His middle brother, Steve, always sat between his parents, close to both of them.

Jesse had never asked him, but, looking back, it seemed as if Steve must have known the divorce was coming. He had always tried to keep the peace, no matter what it took. . . .

Jesse remembered one Saturday in particular, when he was still pretty little and Steve was maybe eleven. The two of them had been trying to make a wooden birdhouse on the deck overlooking the beach while their parents fought indoors. The adults' angry voices had carried clearly through the sliding glass doors, only partly muffled by the sounds of surf and the inexpert pounding of nails.

Steve had finally begun to cry. "I hate it when they fight," he'd said. "I hate it more than anything."

Jesse didn't remember what he'd said, but he'd been seven, so he knew it probably wasn't that helpful. He'd never forget what Steve did next, though. Putting his left hand flat on the wooden railing, his brother had gazed out to sea a long, still moment. Then he'd brought the hammer down hard on his left middle finger.

Jesse was the one who'd screamed.

Both his parents had come running, everything forgotten except Steve's bloody fingertip.

"Oh, Stevie!" his mother had cried, gathering him into her arms. "Oh, baby."

Jesse's doctor father had examined the injured finger as carefully as if it were a broken leg or cancer or something, then had relievedly pronounced it not seriously damaged. He'd ruffled Steven's sun-bleached head, which was still tucked into his mother's shoulder. "You have to be more careful, son. I don't want you boys using tools anymore when I'm not around."

"You were busy, Dad," Steve had sniffed. "And you said we could make the birdhouse *today*."

"Okay. So we'll make it now. I'm not busy anymore."

Mrs. Jones had fussed over her middle son a moment longer, then stood and forced a smile. "You know what? I'm going to fix us all a nice lunch. How will that be? Jesse, run down the beach and find Kevin."

Jesse had started for the stairs to the sand, but not before he'd read the unspoken message in Steve's wet eyes: *It was worth it*. He was sure his parents had never guessed Steven's tears had caused his injury, and not the other way around.

"Hey, Jesse!" Jason hissed suddenly, poking him in the ribs. "You know what? I'll bet people think we're *brothers*."

"Yeah," Jesse whispered, smiling weakly. "Brothers."

113

"Three?" Nicole repeated eagerly. "Sure! Which ones?"

"Oh, I don't know. Why don't you choose for me?" The woman smiled down at the two small children she held by the hands. "I'm a little tied up right now."

"Sure thing!" Nicole scurried to pick three good pumpkins from the piles Eight Prime had set up on the asphalt. Reverend Thompson had told the congregation the sale in the parking lot was to benefit the Junior Explorers, and now that services were over, the makeshift pumpkin patch was mobbed with customers. All the members of Eight Prime were racing around like crazy, selling pumpkins and helping carry them to cars. Nicole almost wished she'd asked Courtney to lend them a hand.

No. What are you thinking? she asked herself as she stood up with a pumpkin in her arms and the tall church steeple caught her eye. *You don't need that kind of abuse.*

She was actually kind of glad that Courtney had already made plans with Jeff. Nicole didn't like feeling as if she were losing her best friend to a guy, but, on the other hand, bringing Courtney to a church—even a church parking lot—was bound to be way more work than reward.

"Can I help you, Nicole?" a shy voice asked.

Nicole looked down to see Melanie's little protégée, Amy, trotting along at her side. "You want to help *me*?" Nicole said, surprised.

"Can I?"

Nicole felt a surge of pity. Amy seemed so sad— smaller, somehow, without Melanie.

"Do you think you can carry this pumpkin to that lady's car? It's heavy." It was actually quite small, or Nicole wouldn't have risked it.

Amy nodded solemnly.

"Okay, then. Be careful." Nicole lowered the gourd into Amy's embrace and the little girl started carefully back to the front of the pumpkin patch, where the woman waited for them. Nicole quickly selected two more, one for each arm, then hurried to catch up.

"What do you think of these three?" Nicole asked her customer.

"Fine," said the woman.

"We're going to carry them to your car," Amy announced.

"Well, I do appreciate that," the woman told her. "Thank you very much."

Amy beamed, and five people and three pumpkins set out across the pavement. Nicole noticed that Peter and Jenna were also loading pumpkins, and Jesse and his buddy Jason walked past them on a return trip. "Hi, Jesse," she called, smiling.

Jesse nodded like Mr. Cool, but he did return her smile.

"Here we are!" the woman said. She let go of her children's hands long enough to pop open the back hatch of her station wagon.

Nicole put her two pumpkins inside, then hurriedly reached for Amy's, lifting that one in as well. "Thanks a lot," she said as she collected the money.

"Thanks for the bus," Amy echoed.

The woman smiled and spoke to Amy. "I'm afraid that's not quite a bus yet, honey. But you hang in there. You'll get it."

Amy nodded. "I know."

Their customer drove off, and Nicole headed back to the pumpkin patch, Amy on her heels.

"Look, Nicole!" Ben greeted her. "We're almost sold out already."

He was right. Pumpkins were flying out of the piles—two to this family, three to that. Even better, lots of people were overpaying and telling Eight Prime to keep the change. Nicole took a spot next to Ben and started selling again. She had just collected for a big one when an elderly lady in a flowered dress handed her ten bucks for nothing.

"Don't you want a pumpkin?" Nicole asked, surprised.

"Heavens, no." The woman laughed. "My pumpkin-carving days are over."

"You might as well take one," Nicole insisted. "I'll carry it to your car."

"Give it to one of your little helpers," the lady

116

suggested, smiling at Elton, who was nearby, helping Ben. Nicole looked around for Amy, but she had drifted off to join Peter.

"All right. Thanks." Nicole grabbed the nearest large pumpkin and set it in the back of Peter's pickup. She'd let him figure out who to give it to later.

"Look at that! Completely empty," Jenna said happily, walking up behind her. She gestured to the truck bed, empty except for Nicole's single pumpkin. "Scratched, rusted metal has never been more beautiful."

Nicole nodded. "You guys have a great congregation."

"Yes, we do," Jenna said. "I'm sure yours is just as nice, though," she added a second later.

Nicole had never really thought about it. "Yeah. I guess they probably are."

A few minutes later, the sale was over. Jenna's parents came over to pick up their five pumpkins, Peter's parents took two, and the last cars trickled out of the parking lot. Eight Prime was alone with only eighteen leftover pumpkins and a handful of Junior Explorers.

"I can't believe we sold them all!" Leah exclaimed.

"Not bad," Miguel agreed. Nicole noticed that Amy was hanging around him now. The poor little girl seemed lost without Melanie's hand to cling to.

"What are we going to do with these?" Ben asked, pointing to the leftovers.

Peter shrugged. "If it's okay with all of you, I'll let the Junior Explorers color them with markers next week and take them home for Halloween."

"Oh, cool!" Priscilla cried excitedly.

"Markers are for babies!" Jason protested almost simultaneously. "Why can't we cut them open and scoop out their guts?"

"Because they won't last until Halloween if you do."

Nicole had to hand it to Peter—the guy always knew exactly the right thing to say.

"I'm going to make mine a clown," Lisa announced decisively.

Of all the Junior Explorers, Lisa was the one Nicole was most drawn to. She was so delicate, so adorable. She looked especially darling that morning in her fancy white dress and shiny blond ringlets. But the girl stuck to Peter like glue, and Nicole knew a desperate crush when she saw one.

"A clown!" Jason snorted. "I'm going to make mine a vampire. With fangs!"

Then the rest of the Junior Explorers started yelling their ideas, all clamoring to speak at the same time. Nicole saw the excitement in their eyes as they struggled to outdo each other, and for the first time since Eight Prime had formed, she felt happy that she'd joined.

118

I'm doing a good thing, she thought, watching the children's faces. They were still trying to one-up each other, their ideas getting more and more outrageous. And suddenly Nicole felt great—*really* great.

In fact, helping these kids is probably the best thing I've ever done.

"So, how did it feel to be in church again?" Leah asked Miguel. They had driven separate cars to the pumpkin sale, and now they lingered behind, talking in the parking lot.

Miguel shrugged. "I never thought I'd have to tell my mother a story to go to church. I feel like a criminal."

"I don't know why you didn't just tell her the truth. You said she was dying to get you back into church."

"Yeah. Into *her* church. I don't know . . . maybe she'd be okay with it. I just don't want to upset her any more." His brows drew into a scowl and his voice took on a touchy tone. "Besides, it's not like I'm converting, or, or reverting, or . . . *anything*. I only came because of the sale."

"Okay," Leah said, eager to change the subject before he got mad. "Should we go off campus for lunch tomorrow, or do you want me to bring lunch from home?"

"Whatever," he said sulkily.

Leah glanced quickly around the deserted parking lot. They were alone. She slipped her arms around him, pressing up close. "How about Burger City? My treat."

Miguel drew back and stared at her suspiciously. "*Your* treat? How come?"

Leah flushed. "I just want to, all right? Can't the girl pay once in a while?"

"I guess so," he said doubtfully.

"All right then. It's a date." She kissed him lightly, her lips barely brushing his. "I'll see you tomorrow." She moved to break the embrace, but Miguel held on.

"You've got to be kidding," he said, a glimmer of humor restored to his eyes. "You call that a kiss?"

"Miguel . . ."

"That's supposed to last me till tomorrow? No, I think you can do better than that." He lowered his mouth to hers, to show her what he had in mind.

"Miguel," she murmured between kisses, "this *is* a church."

"It's the parking lot. Doesn't count."

He was smiling again when Leah drove off in her father's brown Ford. She watched him in her rearview mirror as long as she could, and when she had to turn and couldn't see him anymore, she felt their separation like a physical loss. It was a shortage of air in her lungs, a tightening down in her gut. She loved him so much.

120

She wished she'd never, ever spied on him.

After Miguel had inadvertently ditched her the morning before, Leah had eventually managed to find him. Two streets after she'd figured he'd lost her for good, she'd come up behind him at a light. From there it had become a cat-and-mouse game, following the del Rioses around without being seen herself. They'd gone to the bank, then into a complex of medical and professional buildings, where Leah had endured a long, boring wait parked on the street outside. She couldn't see a thing, and she'd been seriously considering giving up when Miguel and Rosa had suddenly driven out, minus their mother.

Mrs. del Rios must work in one of those buildings, Leah had realized. *They were just dropping her off.* But there had been no time to wonder what Mrs. del Rios's job might be as Leah had scrambled to restart her mom's car and follow Miguel again. His top-secret destination had been the grocery store, and when he and Rosa had finally come back out, Miguel pushing a full cart of groceries, Leah had understood at last what an idiot she'd been. She hadn't even bothered to follow them back to their house. She'd already known who'd be carrying in all the heavy bags.

"You're such a fool," she told herself now, driving home. "What in the world were you thinking?"

She'd been so convinced that Miguel was up to something shady, maybe even something really bad.

Instead her big discovery had been that her new boyfriend was simply a dutiful son—the man of the house now that his father was gone. He was so clearly protective of his mother and sister—opening their doors, insisting on carrying everything. He also appeared to be the family's only driver, and his the only car.

Leah wished she could tell him she knew where he lived and what he did on Saturday mornings, and that she loved him more than ever now. But how could she, when she wasn't supposed to know? Her guilty conscience was driving her crazy, but telling Miguel that she'd spied on him was completely out of the question.

I'd be pretty furious if somebody did that to me, she thought, cringing to imagine how furious. *If I found out Miguel had been sneaking around spying on me and my family, I'd probably be just about mad enough to break up with him on the spot.*

Eight

Melanie tossed her magazine aside on her bed-spread and sighed. She was tired of reading, she was tired of staying home, and she was sick to death of lying down. "I never thought I'd say this," she grumbled, "but I wish I could go back to school."

School was on hold for a couple more days, though. Her father had taken her to see Dr. Levenstein earlier that Monday, and even though everything seemed to be healing fine, the doctor had been concerned that she still had headaches.

"Better to be safe and wait a little longer," he'd said jovially. "A smart girl like you can always catch up."

Catching up was the least of her concerns—dying of boredom was much higher on her list.

"And no cheerleading for a couple of weeks," he'd added. "When you do go back, I want you to take it easy. No games, and no practices."

Melanie couldn't wait to hear what old Vanessa would say about that.

"At least he took the stitches out," she murmured, running a hand through her damp blond hair. The instant she'd gotten back from the doctor's office she'd leapt into the shower for her first good shampooing since the accident. Stubble was already growing on her scalp in the spot the doctor had shaved. She rubbed her fingertips lightly back and forth across it now, shivering at the strange, prickly sensation. The area was about as long as her little finger and twice as wide, but the rest of her thick hair covered it. Once again, Melanie felt grateful to Dr. Levenstein for showing such restraint with the razor.

Swinging her slippered feet off the bed and down to the floor, Melanie stood and tightened the belt of her soft chenille bathrobe. "I think I'll do some painting," she announced. Her voice rang out in the empty room, startling her.

And turn on a radio, she added silently. *I'm starting to talk to myself.*

She left her bedroom and shuffled down the upstairs hall, her slippers a whisper on the cool gray marble. Her father was downstairs fooling around in his office, so she had the whole floor to herself. She reached the far end of the hall, hesitated, then opened the closed door in front of her.

Sunlight assaulted her eyes, flooding into the hall from floor-to-ceiling windows along the back wall of the room she'd just opened—her mother's studio. These days the studio was rarely disturbed by anyone except Mrs. Murphy, the housekeeper.

Mr. Andrews avoided the place on principle, and Melanie hadn't felt comfortable there since her mother's death. When her mom was alive, it had been her sanctuary, a by-invitation-only kind of place. There *had* been invitations, of course—Melanie had learned to paint there. But since her mother's death, Melanie had always felt as if she were intruding whenever she entered the studio. She slipped through the door now and closed it behind her, uncertain whether she should stay and paint there or grab some supplies and go somewhere else.

It would be a lot easier to paint here, she thought. Two massive easels dominated the room, and paints and brushes were easy to reach on a couple of small, rolling carts. Various types of paper filled an enormous flat file, and a series of shuttered cupboards held canvases. Best of all, the concrete floor was already covered with paint, eliminating the need for drop cloths. Mrs. Andrews had firmly believed that was what a studio's floor was for.

"The more the better," she'd often said. "The floor's just a horizontal canvas."

Melanie wandered across that cold canvas now and rested one cheek on a double-paned window. The maples on the Andrewses' large property were ruddy with fall, and the grass was tinged with tawny brown. A bank of clouds skittered across a sharp blue sky, pushed by a breeze from the south. And over in the hollow, Melanie knew, the brook would be getting cold. She closed her eyes and imagined the slick silver water sliding down mossy rocks.

"Mom would have loved to paint this," she whispered.

And then she realized her mind was made up. She turned and pulled a cart to the larger easel and began squeezing watercolors onto a palette. Some of the tubes were caked and dry, but there were so many that had never been opened that she soon had a rainbow of choices. A rummage in the flat files produced white watercolor paper. Melanie clipped a thick sheet to the easel, then went to get some water from the small sink in the corner. The faucet sputtered noisily, spitting air through shuddering pipes, and the first water that gushed out had the slight brown tinge of rust. When the stream finally cleared, Melanie filled a glass and began painting.

Her first attempts weren't good. She didn't know what she wanted to paint. There was an idea down inside her somewhere, but it wasn't clear yet. On top of that, she was out of practice. The paint didn't flow where she wanted it to. Even so, she kept at it doggedly through several sheets of paper. Gradually, with every tiny brushstroke, her skill and confidence returned.

I'll paint something nice for Peter, she decided as

she pulled a used sheet of paper from under the clip and replaced it with a fresh one. *What would he like?*

She rinsed her brush, thought only a second, and began to paint a sky darkening over a quiet field. Blue, gray, and purple covered the upper half of the paper, with a break near the center and color that deepened toward the edges. Melanie silhouetted the grasses and brush of her field using purples, browns, and greens so dark they were almost black. Then, returning to the break she'd left in her sky, she painted streaks of light flooding though the clouds, illuminating an irregular swath of tawny field below. She worked hard at the painting, concentrating on the contrast between light and shadow, and after a while she stood back to survey her work.

It needed something more. She added a pale outcropping of rock and a low rail fence meandering through the field, half in light and half in darkness, throwing shadows on the grass.

That's better. I hope Peter likes it, she thought as she switched to a smaller brush and started working on details. *It'll be nice to do something for him after all he's done for me.*

She remembered the conversation they'd had on Saturday, when she'd told him about the weird things she'd experienced while unconscious. Just the recollection of her accident gave her a strange feeling now, as if she were on borrowed time. Or no, that wasn't it. It was more as if she were on *new* time, as if her life could be divided into everything that had happened before the accident and everything to come.

"That's a little overdramatic," she muttered, stroking some shadows into the grass. Still . . . it was how she felt. Everything was changing. She wasn't sure why—she wasn't sure what it was changing to—but she felt the difference all the same. She wasn't the same girl who'd started school in September full of a two-year-old heartache. Not exactly the same girl, anyway.

Anyone who needed evidence of that could have eavesdropped on her and Peter on Saturday. Melanie still couldn't believe she'd asked to go to his church—she had no idea what had made her blurt that out. She'd never go, of course. It was just that sometimes, when she talked to Peter, God almost seemed to make sense. Almost. And even when she didn't believe what he said, there was something about the perfect faith in Peter's eyes that made her feel like maybe things weren't as bad as she'd thought.

She liked it when they talked alone.

And then a sudden, bizarre idea stopped her paintbrush in midair. *Am I falling for this guy?*

It had been so long since she'd given a guy a second thought, and now here was Peter, practically under her nose. . . . Could he have slipped by her defenses somehow?

A second later she laughed. *That'll be the day,* she

thought, returning to her painting. *Me and Peter? There probably weren't two more different people in all of Clearwater Crossing. She liked Peter, sure. She liked him a lot. But not like* that. *The two of them together would be a total freak of nature.*

Now, Peter and Jenna are the perfect *couple,* she thought, adding sharp yellow highlights to her autumn leaves. *It's weird that they've been friends all these years and never figured it out.*

"No! No, I can't believe it!" Coach Davis yelled disgustedly as the football slipped through Jesse's hands and hit the grass again. "I could go over to the elementary school right now and find fifth-grade boys who could do it better. Or fifth-grade *girls*, for that matter."

A few of the Wildcats snickered, and Jesse felt lower than the tips of his cleats. *I shouldn't have skipped practice last Friday,* he thought as he trotted back to try the drill again. *I knew I was playing like garbage.*

He'd known it, but he still didn't understand why. Football had always been so easy for him. He'd played brilliantly ever since Pop Warner, and when he'd come to Clearwater Crossing, he'd totally wowed everyone. Coach Davis had predicted great things for him, and the season opener had seemed to prove the coach right.

But that was then. Jesse's second game had been awful. What was even scarier was that he hadn't been able to shake it off. Instead of improving, he seemed to get worse every time he touched a ball. And the way he'd played so far *today*—

The whistle shrilled. "Ready?" shouted the coach. "Go!"

Jesse began to run, flying at top speed across the close-cropped grass. He was supposed to go out long, cut to his left, then turn and catch the ball Hank fired down the field. And the coach was right: It was an easy drill. Grade-school stuff. If he didn't get it right this time, he'd look like a total moron.

His heart pounded as he ran, more from anxiety than effort, and he hoped his hands wouldn't be too sweaty to grip the ball. He reached the end of his straightaway and cut left. Just a few more steps; then he'd turn around and—

Bam! The football hit him in the helmet, just behind his ear. He was so stunned that for a moment he almost didn't realize what had happened. Then he looked down at the markers on the field, gauged his distance from the sidelines, and realized what had gone wrong. He'd overrun. Hank was aiming for a predetermined spot on the field, and Jesse had run right through it.

"What do you think you're doing, Jones?" Coach Davis screamed, beside himself with frustration.

"Hel-*loooo*! We're playing football here! Get off the field and let one of the freshmen show you how it's done."

He waved Jesse off and pointed to Eric Spenser, who was actually a second-string sophomore. Eric and Jesse changed places.

The whistle blew. "Ready? Go!"

Eric streaked down the field, cut left, turned, and caught the ball perfectly. Not the least hesitation, not the least bobble. He made it look exactly as easy as it was. The Wildcats cheered sarcastically from the sidelines, relieved to finally see some progress, and Jesse dropped his eyes to the grass at his feet, humiliated. He just didn't understand it. He was trying so *hard*.

"Looks to me like someone's gunning for your position, Jones," Nate Kilriley said vindictively, sidling up behind him. "The way you're playing, he deserves it, too."

"Shut up, Nate," Jesse growled, wishing he could add some physical persuasion to his request. Nate had been begging for a fight all semester.

"I suppose you're going to make me," Nate retorted, knowing full well Jesse couldn't do anything in front of the coach.

Jesse glared into Nate's piggy little eyes, holding the stare until the other boy turned and walked away. But when Nate had finally gone, Jesse's gaze returned to his shoes. Between leaving his real life behind in California and making Melanie hate him, football was all he had left. If he lost his position on the team . . .

"Okay, Eric. Let's see you run that same play with interference." The coach chose a couple of guys to cover Eric, to prevent him from catching the ball. The duo ran out, the whistle blew, and the second drill began.

Eric ran with confidence, acting as if the two large defenders weren't even there. Hank threw the ball high and Eric turned and leapt for it, snatching it neatly from Dennis Peterson, who was trying to intercept.

"That's the way!" the coach shouted. "Finally! Let's see it one more time."

Jesse watched miserably as Eric lined up to make a fool of him again.

I'm not sure how much more of this I can take, he thought, feeling more pathetic by the minute. *If I survive this practice, I'm going to need a drink.*

Jenna opened the Conrads' front door on Monday afternoon, filled with nervous anticipation. She climbed the first flight of steps, the steps to her old room, then kept walking past her old door, down the landing hall, and up the second flight to the third floor. It was her first day coming home to her new room, and she reached hesitantly for the doorknob, almost afraid to turn it.

What if Caitlin changed her mind and moved back in while I was at school? Or what if Maggie snuck in and messed things up to try to be funny?

But when the door swung open, it revealed a perfect room. Her bed was neatly made with the pastel comforter Caitlin had left her, her things were where she'd put them, and the lilac curtains stirred slightly, framing her new view of nothing but treetops.

"Oh, wow," she whispered softly. It felt more like living on another planet than only one floor up in the same old house.

She moved to her bed, where she dropped her backpack out of habit. Then she picked it up again and took it over to her desk. In her old room, her desk had been so small and cramped that she'd rarely worked there, preferring to spread things out on her bed instead. But her new, built-in desk was enormous, with bookshelves all around it and— best of all—no nosy little sister sneaking up behind it. *On a desk like this, homework might seem almost pleasant*, she thought.

She kicked off her shoes, unzipped her pack, and removed her assignments, arranging the books and papers into piles. Then she hung her empty pack on the back of the chair and sat down to work. She had barely opened her geometry book, however, when a wonderful new idea occurred to her. Rising hurriedly, she walked to the nightstand by her bed, switched on her clock radio, and turned up the volume. She and Maggie had had so many fights about what station to listen to over the years that they'd long since given up having any music at all. With a happy sigh, Jenna sank back into her desk chair, completely ready to do her homework.

She sailed through geometry like a pro, and she was sure she had never understood her biology reading so well. Within an hour, all that was left was a one-page paper for Mr. Smythe, her wannabe-British English teacher. Jenna was so thrilled to be working at her new desk that she'd have given anything to write the paper out by hand, but Mr. Smythe accepted only typed papers. Period.

I suppose I ought to be glad I have a PC at home, she thought as she gathered her essay notes, thinking of the kids who had to stay late at school and wait to use one in the library. *Besides, after this I'll be finished with my homework, and when dinner is over I can come back up and hang my posters, or practice my guitar, or read a book, or . . . anything I want!* She took one last, satisfied look around her new room, then started downstairs to use the computer in the den.

On her way there, she decided to stop by and see how Caitlin and Sarah were doing. Maggie and Allison were acting as if they ruled the house—those two couldn't be happier—but Jenna hadn't heard a thing from the first floor yet that day. She wondered whether Caitlin had settled in.

"Hi! How's it going?" Jenna asked, walking through her sisters' open door. "Oh! You got everything set up!"

Unlike Jenna, who had slaved every free hour of the weekend to fix up her room the way she wanted, or even Allison, who had thrown most of her junk underneath her new bed and called it home, Caitlin had taken her time unpacking her boxes. Sunday evening she was still only halfway done, but then, instead of finishing, she'd spent the evening reading her Bible, keeping to the schedule she'd set to read it from cover to cover within one year. Jenna hadn't been able to understand how Caitlin could sleep with things in that state, but now the answer seemed obvious. Her sister had time to burn, and it had to be easier to unpack while Sarah was at school.

"Pretty cool, huh?" Sarah bragged. "It's *much* more grown up than when Allison was here." She said it with a straight face, apparently unaware that her side of the room was still littered with toys and stuffed animals.

Caitlin's side was as neat as always, although the space was so much smaller than what she'd had that Jenna wondered how she'd found room for all her things. *There must be stuff underneath the bed,* she realized, feeling a little guilty. Still, it wasn't as if *she'd* never had to keep things under the bed.

"Your pictures look nice there," she said quickly, focusing on the positive. She nodded toward the two framed prints on Caitlin's wall.

"Yeah, not bad," Caitlin agreed amiably.

"And look at our closet!" Sarah volunteered, running to slide the doors first to one side, then to the other. The difference between the two wardrobes was impossible to miss. Sarah's little girl's clothes hung down a couple of feet from the bar, while Caitlin's pants and dresses stretched nearly to the floor. "Caitlin's going to let me wear some of her stuff sometimes . . . you know, for special occasions."

That ought to be interesting, Jenna thought, visualizing Sara lost in the folds of Caitlin's too-large clothes. "How fun!" was what she said.

"Yeah, and she's going to help me with my homework, too."

"Good. Well . . . and speaking of homework, I'd better get back to mine. See you guys at dinner." Jenna smiled and began to back out of the room, her sense of guilt growing stronger with each word Sarah said.

"Wait!" Caitlin called. "I have something for you."

"For me?"

Caitlin leaned forward and pulled a medium-sized package from underneath her bed. "It's nothing, really," she said shyly, holding it out to Jenna. "Just a little room-warming present. I thought maybe you could use it."

"Cat! You got me a present? What for?"

"Open it. You'll see."

Jenna hesitated only a second, then rushed forward to grab the gift, sitting on the floor to rip off the wrapping. Inside the carefully taped paper was a brand-new cordless telephone.

"You bought me a phone!" she cried, unable to believe her good luck. "Caitlin! Why?"

Her sister shrugged a little, her cheeks a brilliant pink. "There was a phone in the room when Mary Beth and I moved in, but we decided she should take it to college. It only seems fair to replace it now."

"I can't believe you did this!" Jenna stood up and bent to hug her sister. "I thought you didn't have any money!"

"There's a big difference between enough for a phone and enough for an apartment," Caitlin replied, sounding like someone who knew. "Besides, I found a good sale. Do you like it?"

"Like it? I love it! Thanks, Cat." She gave her sister one last squeeze. "I'm going to set it up right now!"

Her English paper forgotten, Jenna raced back up the stairs with her new telephone. She set the box on her desk, opened it, and pulled out the installation instructions, nearly too excited to read. She still couldn't believe that Caitlin had bought her a phone! Especially after going without one for so long herself. It was almost too generous.

I'll have to do something nice for her, too, Jenna thought, wondering what her sister might like.

In her mind's eye, Jenna saw the room she'd just run out of—Caitlin's side neat and mature, Sarah's like something from *Sesame Street.* Before she could stop it, that creeping sense of guilt overtook her again. There was something not quite right about an eighteen-year-old rooming with a ten-year-old.

But they seem happy enough, she reassured herself quickly, searching for a phone jack near the bed. *Besides, Caitlin's home all day while the rest of us go to school. Five days a week she not only has that room to herself, she has practically the whole house.*

She found the jack and plugged in the base for her new phone. *I will not feel guilty,* she vowed, reading the next step in the instructions. *Caitlin volunteered to move down there, and I will not feel guilty.*

It sounded completely reasonable.

So why did she feel guilty anyway?

Nine

No one is looking at you. You do not look stupid, Nicole told herself over and over as she pretended to read a tattered copy of *Adventures of Huckleberry Finn* for her American novel class. So far she didn't much like it, but she knew there was no way she was getting out of reading Mark Twain in the man's home state. Besides, it gave her a reason to sit in the library by herself, since her supposed friend Courtney had deserted her again in favor of another off-campus lunch with Jeff.

So what else is new? Nicole thought, flipping a page to maintain the illusion that she was reading. Courtney deserted her all the time lately. *I hope she doesn't back out of going to the U.S. Girls contest this Saturday!* Nicole hadn't been wild about the idea of taking Courtney at first, but now, with the modeling contest only days away and Leah and Jenna coming, Nicole needed the security of her best friend.

Of course, she'll probably just make fun of me the entire time, she thought. *There's nothing Court loves more than an audience. I suppose if she has to—*

"Hey, Nicole. How's it going?" Jesse whispered loudly, dropping into the chair across the table.

Nicole looked up from her book in amazement. She knew Jesse wasn't in the habit of spending lunchtime in the library, and she didn't see any books in his hands. Could it be . . . was it possible . . . could he have come there looking for *her*?

The week before had started so well. Jesse had sat with her during lunch on both Tuesday and Wednesday. But on Thursday he hadn't shown up. She hadn't even seen him around, and at the pumpkin sales on Friday and Sunday, he had barely spoken, let alone offered an explanation for his absence. Monday he'd been missing in action again, and Nicole had begun to think that maybe she'd done something wrong. . . .

"I didn't see you in the quad. Not eating today?" Jesse asked.

"I, uh, well, I already ate," Nicole lied, putting down *Huckleberry Finn*. "And then I had some reading to do, so I thought I'd come in here." It *did* sound as if he'd missed her! She was so excited she could barely concentrate.

You'd better *concentrate*, some slightly calm cell in her brain let her know. *If you don't want to chase him away again, you'd better be as cool to him as Melanie always is.*

The idea appealed to her. She lifted her nose an inch and leaned back in her chair. "So, what are you doing here?"

Jesse made a face. "I have to check out a book for one of my classes, and it's easier to do now than after school. What with football practice and everything."

Which would mean that he *hadn't* come looking for her.

"What do you think our chances are against Hickory Hills this Friday?" she asked, feeling totally deflated.

Jesse shrugged as if barely interested. "I've never seen them play, so I don't know."

His lack of enthusiasm surprised her. "Yes, but you must have heard things. I mean, we killed 'em last year. What does Coach Davis say?"

"Coach Davis!" Jesse snorted. "Coach Davis wouldn't give us odds if we were playing senior citizens. He always acts like we'll get our tails whipped, no matter what. He thinks it builds character."

Nicole giggled, then covered her mouth and glanced at the librarian. The woman was busy behind her desk, ignoring everything else.

"We'll beat them," Nicole whispered, lowering her voice. "We always beat them."

Jesse shrugged again and changed the subject. "So how about that pumpkin sale? I think we did pretty good."

"Yes," Nicole agreed. "I can't wait to hear what the final profit was at the meeting this Thursday."

"Is there a meeting Thursday?" Jesse seemed surprised.

"Well . . . yeah. At Jenna's house. Didn't you hear Peter announce it after the sale?"

"I guess not. Maybe I wasn't paying attention."

Nicole found it incredible that he could have missed something so important when he'd been standing right there, but of course she didn't say so. "Peter's going to give us a treasury report, and then we're all supposed to come up with ideas for our next fund-raiser."

"Oh boy!" Jesse said sarcastically. "I was hoping maybe we could take a whole week off for once."

Nicole smiled weakly. "Well, I guess everyone's eager to get the bus."

"Yeah. I guess." He gazed off across the library, a strange, vacant look on his face.

What's wrong with him today? Nicole wondered. *He seems so down.* The second she asked herself the question, though, she thought she knew the answer. *He's missing Melanie, I'll bet.* The mere idea disgusted her.

Still, Melanie was out of the equation—at least for now. And if everything Jesse had told her was true, it could be a good long time before those two were speaking again. He couldn't be expecting much when Melanie came back.

If he was, would he be here talking to me? And despite his excuse about needing a book, he hadn't made the least attempt to look for one. A shrewd look entered Nicole's eyes. Maybe he was starting to take her seriously after all.

He certainly has nothing to lose.

Her breathing sped up at the thought, but she did her best to prevent her excitement from showing. She couldn't lose her head now—she had to keep absolutely cool.

Because the truth was that, in spite of everything, she still liked Jesse Jones. In fact, she liked him more than ever.

She just didn't trust him a bit.

"Wow!" Jenna exclaimed as Peter pulled his Toyota up the Andrewses' driveway. "Not rich at all, are they?" She had never been to Melanie's house before, and she found the enormous glass-and-concrete structure more than a tad overwhelming.

"Money isn't everything," Peter said, shutting off the engine. "Where Melanie's concerned, I don't think it's even very much."

Jenna nodded as they climbed out of the car. Peter was right—Melanie didn't seem particularly impressed with her money. She never mentioned it, and aside from her clothes, it was hard to tell she was even well off. Jenna certainly hadn't guessed she was *this* well off. She followed Peter up to the door, where he knocked on the smooth white wood.

"You did tell her we were coming, right?" Jenna asked, wondering how anyone would hear their knock in that enormous place. "Maybe we should ring the bell."

Peter shrugged, but as he reached for the doorbell, the door opened. "Hey! Hello, Peter," Mr. Andrews said. "And you must be . . ."

"Jenna," she supplied. She had been introduced to Melanie's father at the hospital, but under the circumstances she wasn't too surprised that he didn't remember.

"Jenna. Of course. Melanie's in her room. Go on up." He opened the door wider and waved toward a curving gray marble staircase. "Take two lefts when you get to the landing."

Jenna followed Peter up the stairs, almost afraid to put her weight down lest her footsteps echo in that hollow place. Large framed watercolors covered the raw concrete wall on her right, making the space feel more like a museum than a house. At last they reached the landing, where huge plate glass windows overlooked a giant rectangular swimming pool, poolhouse, and the woods beyond. Jenna barely caught a glimpse before they turned left down a hall, then left again, stopping at an open doorway.

"Hello!" Peter called, rapping on its frame. "Melanie?"

"Come on in," Melanie's voice replied from somewhere inside.

They walked through the doorway, and Jenna gasped. Melanie's bedroom was twice as big as the

Conrads' living room! Melanie was standing by her queen-sized bed, dressed in jeans and a fuzzy pink sweater and looking like a cheerleading legend again. She even had a tan. As Peter and Jenna crossed the room, she hurriedly slapped a stick-on bow on something lying flat on the bed.

"Hi!" she said. "I'm afraid I wasn't as quick as I thought I'd be. I meant to have this ready before you got here." She shrugged charmingly. "Oh, well. Ta-da!"

Holding up the item under the bow, Melanie turned it toward them then shyly extended it toward Peter. "It's for you, Peter. I hope you like it."

"For me? What for?" Dumbfounded, Peter took the framed print of a cloudy meadow and stared.

Melanie colored slightly. "I just . . . wanted to thank you, I guess. For being there for me. In the ambulance and everything."

"But this is too much!" Peter protested. "You didn't have to do this."

"I wanted to. Besides, we have tons of art stuff and empty frames just lying around. It wasn't any big deal."

Jenna's eyes widened as she finally understood. "You mean you *painted* that?" She took the picture from Peter, holding it up to get a better look. "Wow! I thought it was a print."

Melanie laughed. "I wish! It's not that good."

"*I* think it's pretty good!" Jenna said. Peter had

once mentioned that Melanie knew how to paint, but she'd had no idea . . .

"It's beautiful," said Peter. "Thanks, Melanie."

"I thought maybe you could hang it in your room," Melanie suggested, obviously pleased that he liked it.

"I will." Peter took the painting back from Jenna. "I know just where I'll put it, too."

The three of them stood there awkwardly a moment, out of things to say.

"Why don't we go down to the kitchen and get a soda or something?" said Melanie. "I'm sure you don't want to hang around up here." She gestured to her room as if it weren't good enough for company, even though by then Jenna had noticed that it boasted a private bathroom and a walk-in closet.

"Here is fine. Downstairs is fine," Peter said amiably.

Jenna glanced his way, unable to suppress a twinge of annoyance. He sounded as if Melanie had merely to command and he would obey. It would have been kind of nauseating under the best of circumstances, but it was especially so when he was still barely giving Jenna the time of day.

"I love your room," Jenna said to distract herself. She walked across the pristine white carpet to the wide picture windows and gazed out over the front of the Andrewses' acreage. "That's some view."

Melanie smiled only slightly, as if the sight used to interest her once but didn't anymore. "Thanks."

"And is that a walk-in closet?"

"Yeah. Take a look, if you like."

It seemed strange to look into someone else's closet, but Jenna couldn't resist. She left Melanie and Peter discussing the fine points of Peter's new painting and quietly opened the louvered white doors. Inside, the space was even bigger than she'd imagined—more like a walk-in *room* than a closet— with special rods and drawers and shoe compartments, and a virtual department store full of clothes. She withdrew her head hastily, but gave in to the temptation to peek into Melanie's bathroom— white marble, gold fixtures, beveled mirrors . . .

"Are you ready?" Melanie called. Jenna spun around to see that she and Peter had both moved to the doorway. "Let's go downstairs."

Jenna followed silently as Melanie led the way down the marble steps, strangely put out by the luxury of her surroundings. She knew it was petty and wrong to care about money, especially when she didn't lack for things herself, but that only made her feel worse.

Don't be such a spoiled baby, she lectured herself as they walked single file to the kitchen. *So what if Melanie's room is nicer—all right, a lot nicer—than yours? Yesterday you thought your room was great.* Still, when she remembered now how she'd begged and pestered and cajoled to get it, she felt a little foolish. *Melanie* had a room.

They reached the Andrewses' gourmet kitchen and Melanie opened the door of an industrial-looking stainless-steel refrigerator. "What would you like to drink, Peter?" she asked with a big smile. "I think we have just about everything."

Yeah. No kidding, Jenna thought glumly.

"Anything's fine," Peter replied in the same too-nice voice he'd adopted upstairs. "Whatever's closest."

And that was when Jenna realized that it wasn't the room that was bugging her. Not entirely, anyway. What she really wanted to know was how come Melanie and Peter were acting like best friends all of a sudden?

Melanie handed Peter a Coke, then took a diet drink for herself. "How about you, Jenna?"

"Whatever's closest," Jenna echoed, somehow managing to keep the sarcasm out of her voice.

They carried their drinks into the sitting area on the other side of the breakfast bar, where more windows looked out across the patio to the pool.

"I'm coming back to school tomorrow," Melanie told them as they sat down on the pale leather furniture. "You won't have to make any more sympathy calls on poor little me."

"Like we minded!" Peter scoffed. "We've all been really worried about you. Haven't we, Jenna?"

"We have," she agreed. Still, she wished Peter wouldn't make such a big deal about it. All the members of Eight Prime were relieved that Melanie was all right. Why did Peter have to sound as if he were somehow doubly so?

Melanie smiled—at Peter. "How was the sale at your church? Did you count the money yet?"

Jenna stewed in silence as Peter rattled off more details than any human being could possibly want to know. It seemed as if the two of them barely even knew she was there anymore, and it was wearing pretty thin.

You're jealous, a voice in her head whispered.

Am not! she replied immediately. *Of what?*

Peter's paying more attention to Melanie than he is to you.

Well, that *was* kind of annoying, she had to admit. After all, he was her best friend, not Melanie's.

What if they like each other?

Oh, please! Now, that's just ridiculous.

In fact, Jenna could barely keep from laughing at the idea. Hadn't Peter already assured her he had no romantic interest in Melanie? And that was even assuming they had anything in common, which they didn't.

Jesse's much more Melanie's type, she thought. *Or even Miguel.*

Miguel. Every time she thought of him, it still hurt like nothing else.

149

Ten

"I thought they shaved part of your head!" Tiffany objected, her voice heavy with disappointment. It was Wednesday, and the cheerleaders were sitting at their usual lunchtime table, Melanie back in their midst. "You can't even see it!"

"They did a good job," Melanie replied sweetly, thinking something not nearly so nice.

"You look great," Tanya said. "No one would even know."

"No one would know *except* that you're missing the game this Friday," Vanessa put in. "I don't know what we're going to do about that." Her words were harsh, as always, but her tone was actually human. Melanie turned to her, surprised.

"What do you think we ought to do?" Vanessa asked. "Should we assign new positions and try to close up the gap? Or should we just do everything the same and leave a hole where you'd usually be?"

"You're asking *me*?" Melanie replied, stunned.

Vanessa shrugged. "If you have an opinion."

"Well . . . I guess close up the gap. It'll look better."

"Are you sure you won't mind? I mean, it's not like we're forgetting you or anything. In fact, it would be great if you'd dress and come out to the bench, so everyone can see you're all right."

"Okay," Melanie agreed. This was a whole new side of Vanessa. She was being almost . . . nice.

Vanessa nodded, then turned to the others. "Okay. Obviously we aren't going to do the spirit pyramid, or any of the other stunts involving Melanie. When we do the first dance, I'm going to put Cindy . . ."

Melanie tuned her squad leader out as she issued instructions to the other girls. Whatever they decided didn't really affect her—she'd just be sitting on the sidelines. Instead, her thoughts turned to Peter and Jenna, and their visit the day before.

Peter seemed to like the painting, she thought, remembering the way he'd smiled when she'd given it to him. *I wonder if he hung it up yet, and whether it looks good in his room.*

For that matter, she was kind of curious to know what his room looked like. *Maybe I can check it out at the Eight Prime meeting tomorrow,* she thought. Everyone always stayed in the living room, but this time she had a good reason to ask to see his bedroom. If she got there early enough . . .

Oh, wait, she remembered. *The meeting is at Jenna's house this week.*

She sighed, disappointed. Some other time.

151

Jesse leaned against the wall inside the entrance to the cafeteria, his eyes on Melanie. She was finally back, sitting at a table with the other cheerleaders.

Just walk over there and talk to her, he told himself. But he didn't move. He hadn't seen Melanie since that one early visit in the hospital, and he wasn't sure how she'd react to him now.

After all, she did tell you to leave her alone. She could go completely ballistic. The possibility, however slim, was enough to freeze him in place. Considering the grief he'd put up with from the Wildcats lately, Jesse didn't feel like he could take any more rejection—humiliation in front of the entire cheerleading squad was completely out of the question.

On the other hand, what were his options? A few of the Wildcats were sitting at a nearby table. He could push in there and eat with them. But even assuming they gave him a break and didn't mention the terrible way he'd been playing—which was basically hoping for miracles—he couldn't bear to hear them sing Eric Spenser's praises one more time. The way things were going, that guy was becoming a serious threat.

Disgusted by his own indecision, Jesse finally pushed off from the wall and slunk out the door to the quad. He cut across the corner to the nearest classroom building, then walked down the empty hall to the boys' room.

The air inside the bathroom reeked of stale cigarettes, and a couple of hard-looking guys sat smoking on the ancient radiator, adding to the stench. Jesse ignored them and locked himself into the nearest stall. Hanging his backpack on a hook on the door, he reached in and pulled a small metal flask from its depth—straight vodka.

The odor as he uncapped it bit his nostrils, but by now he knew better than to smell. He held his breath and brought the flask to his lips, gulping down half its contents.

I could drink off the rest right now, no problem, he thought, wishing it were possible. If he did, though, there wouldn't be anything left for after practice— and he had a feeling he'd need it worse then. Reluctantly recapping the flask, he dropped it into his pack and closed the zipper.

"I didn't hear any toilet flush," one of the toughs observed as Jesse opened the door and walked back out of the stall. The two of them sniggered as if they knew exactly what he'd been doing.

"Yeah? What kind of freak listens to other guys in the john?" Jesse pushed out the swinging door without waiting for an answer, wondering if the pair would come after him. He actually half hoped they would. But no one ran up behind him in the empty hallway, and a moment later he was back in the quad, already feeling somewhat better.

Hey! There's Nicole.

153

Jesse started walking toward her bench. At least Nicole was always glad to see him—unlike Melanie. When he'd stumbled across her in the library the day before, she'd lit up like she'd won the lottery.

"Hey, Nicole. How's it going?" he asked, sliding in beside her. He could feel the alcohol doing its work . . . loosening his muscles, loosening his tongue.

"Hi, Jesse!" Nicole looked up immediately, dropping her book and widening her turquoise eyes for his benefit. It killed him the way she always did that—as if it were possible to miss eyes that color.

"Still reading that same book?" he asked, gesturing to *Huckleberry Finn*.

"It's so boring," she complained. "It's totally for guys."

"It *is* kind of for guys, I guess," he said, feeling suddenly magnanimous. "I used to like it when I was a kid."

Nicole beamed.

"So, how come you're all alone today? Where's Courtney?"

"Off with Jeff again," she replied, the smile fading from her face. "Sometimes it feels like I don't even have a best friend anymore."

"I guess you'd rather sit with Courtney than with me, then," Jesse teased, trying out one of his more flirty looks.

The effect was instantaneous. "No!" Nicole said

loudly. Her cheeks flushed, and she lowered her voice. "I mean, no. Don't be silly."

Jesse stifled a laugh. Nicole tried so hard to be cool around him—and it was obviously such a big effort. He wondered how she endured the strain.

She's such a little girl compared to Melanie, he thought. *Everything shows. Everything's on the outside.* No matter how hard she tried not to, she gave herself away.

"So you don't mind if I stay, then?" He couldn't resist toying with her.

"Of course not. I mean, uh, anything's better than reading *Huckleberry Finn.*" Her face was as pink as a tropical shell.

"Okay," he said, slouching down more comfortably and imagining how differently Melanie would have handled the situation.

That was the thing he admired most about Melanie—her complete and total self-control. *A bomb could go off in the quad, and Melanie wouldn't even blink,* he thought, smiling at the idea. The only time he'd ever seen her break was when Kurt Englbehrt had died and she'd lost it in the cafeteria. That whole thing had happened so fast, though, and everyone had been so stunned. Sometimes he wondered if it had really happened at all. It seemed so impossible . . . so completely out of character.

"Are you ready for the game this Friday?" Nicole asked with a chipper smile.

Oh, no, she's going to try football again, Jesse groaned to himself. He wished she'd add a few new subjects to her repertoire. Still, it wasn't a bad change of pace to hang out with a girl like Nicole—someone who actually let you know what she was thinking.

I could do worse, he thought. Besides, such blatant adoration was doing wonders for his ego.

"Can you pass me that book?" Miguel whispered to Leah, pointing to a volume on her side of the table.

They were in their favorite on-campus hiding place—behind the book stacks in the CCHS library—pretending to work on their homework, but way too many extraneous requests for books and pencils and notes to be passed were being made for anything useful to get accomplished. It didn't matter. They both knew they were only there to be together. The real homework would get done later, after they went home.

"This book?" Leah teased, pointing to the only one he could possibly mean. "You want me to pass *this* book?"

"If it's not too much trouble."

Leah turned to reach for the book. Miguel immediately seized the opportunity to tickle her, going for the sliver of bare skin under her ribs, where her short sweater separated from the waistband of her skirt.

"Ooh! You're asking for it!" she giggled, squirming away from him. She pushed her chair backward, but as she did its metal legs made a horrendous squawking sound on the old linoleum tiles. They both froze, then hurriedly buried their noses in books at different ends of the table. Leah's heart pounded as she waited for the librarian, or a teacher, or even a curious fellow student to come see what the commotion was.

No one did. After a few minutes Miguel scooted back to her side, being careful to lift his chair instead of sliding it. "Way to go, Rosenthal," he whispered, his voice full of mirth. "Way to be sly."

"Pass me that book," she replied petulantly, pointing.

He fell for it. The second he reached across the table, Leah went for his ribs. He spun around and grabbed her hands, pushing them under the table. They both stifled laughter as she tried desperately to free herself to resume her tickling.

"Hey, what are you two doing back here?" a friendly voice asked from behind them.

Miguel let go of her instantly. Leah turned her head, horrified to see Melanie Andrews smiling down on them, a load of books in her arms.

"I didn't think anyone knew about this place but me," Melanie whispered, taking a seat on Leah's other side. "It's usually completely dead back here."

"Yes, well, we were just studying," Leah replied,

her pulse racing so fast she could feel something throb on the side of her throat. Melanie couldn't have shown up at a worse time. Amazingly though, she was just sitting there, smiling as if everything were perfectly normal. Was it possible she hadn't noticed Leah and Miguel holding hands? "We've got biology together," Leah added weakly.

Melanie nodded. "I barely even *know* what I've got anymore. I have so much work to make up, it's not even funny."

That's it! Leah realized. Melanie must have been so distracted by her books that she hadn't noticed Leah and Miguel fooling around under the table.

"So how are you feeling now?" Leah asked, daring to breathe again. "Better?"

"Yeah. I'm fine. How about you guys? Anything interesting happen while I was gone?" Melanie looked at Miguel.

"Same old, same old," he said hurriedly. His voice sounded reasonably normal, but he darted a nervous glance at Leah. "You know what? I'm going to go look for a book I need before they close up and kick us out of here. I'll see you girls tomorrow." He gathered his things in a rush, not even putting them into his backpack before he walked away.

"Bye," Leah whispered after him, wishing he weren't leaving. Maybe it was best, though, under the circumstances.

"Bye," Melanie echoed tamely. But Miguel was barely out of earshot before her demeanor changed completely.

"So when did *you* two happen?" she demanded, turning to Leah with an enormous game-day grin. "I wasn't unconscious *that* long."

"I, uh, what do you mean?"

"Oh, please. You're *so* busted." Melanie glanced back over her shoulder in the direction Miguel had gone. "I always thought he was totally cute," she confided, returning her gaze to Leah. "But I guess he's off the market now."

Leah was panicking. Possible excuses raced through her head, but everything sounded so lame. "We were only studying . . . ," she began.

"Really? Maybe I'll ask him out, then. A cutie like Miguel? It's a shame to let so much talent go to waste."

Leah tried to shrug like she didn't care, but then her eyes locked with Melanie's and she had to concede defeat. The game was over.

"All right. You caught us," Leah admitted reluctantly. "But could you please, *please* keep this to yourself? We aren't ready to go public yet."

"Does the rest of Eight Prime know?" Melanie asked curiously.

"No. No one knows. Well . . . my parents do. But they're the only ones."

"If your parents know, then Miguel's must too."

"No—just don't ask," Leah added quickly as Melanie opened her mouth to follow up on that one.

Melanie smiled. "Well, *I* think it's romantic that you're keeping it a secret. Most girls couldn't wait to brag about bagging Miguel del Rios."

"I haven't exactly *bagged* him," Leah said, raising her sculpted brows. "I'm not even sure I want to know what that means."

"Actually, there are a variety of possible meanings," Melanie teased. "But anyway, congratulations. I'm happy for you."

"Really?"

"Sure. I know we don't really know each other that well, but I think the two of you make a good couple."

"And you aren't going to tell anyone. Right?"

A strange, slightly sad look flitted across Melanie's face. "Don't worry," she said. "No one keeps a secret better than I do."

Eleven

Nicole paced her bedroom in a panic, nothing but a white towel wrapped around her. Jesse was going to pick her up for the Eight Prime meeting any minute, and she still didn't know what to wear!

He had called toward the end of dinner. Nicole had seized the excuse of the ringing telephone to abandon her barely touched plate. *It's probably Courtney,* she'd thought, hurrying into the kitchen. *She knows I have Eight Prime tonight, so she's decided tonight is the night we just* have *to do something together.*

She had almost forgotten to breathe when Jesse's voice had come over the line. "Hey, Nicole. Is that you?"

"Yes," she'd managed to get out somehow. He had never called her house before. She hadn't even known he had her number.

"I was wondering if you need a ride to the meeting tonight. If you want, I can swing by and pick you up."

"Okay." Her father had already agreed to let

her drive his Honda, but there was clearly no comparison.

"See you around seven-fifteen?"

Seven-fifteen. Nicole stopped pacing long enough to glance anxiously at the clock on her nightstand. It was now exactly two minutes before seven-fifteen, and she wasn't even dressed.

"Put on some underwear," she told herself, speaking aloud in her nervousness. "You at least know you're going to wear that."

She hadn't been planning to shower before the Eight Prime meeting, or wash and style her hair, or do her very best makeup, either, but she'd raced to do all those things the second she'd hung up the phone. Now she was running late. She dropped the towel, hurriedly put on some underthings, and threw her closet door open wide. The red-white-and-blue U.S. Girls shopping bag on the top shelf immediately caught her eye.

"Perfect!" she whispered, reaching for it. She jerked the pristine new jeans from the bag and ripped off the tags with a shaking hand. Then, holding her breath for luck, she stepped into the legs and pulled them up. The pants were tight, but they slid up fairly easily—much more easily than when she'd bought them. With trembling fingers, she buttoned the fly and adjusted the buckle at the small of her back.

They fit!

Rushing to the full-length mirror on the back of her bathroom door, she checked the view from every angle. She could barely believe that she had the jeans on, or how very thin she was.

Even so, they were still pretty tight. She didn't want to look as if someone had poured her into them at the modeling contest on Saturday.

Don't worry, they'll stretch, she reassured herself quickly. *Wear them tonight, and tomorrow after school. If you don't wash them before the contest—*

The doorbell rang. Nicole leapt away from the mirror and ran to her window. It was Jesse! She could just make out his red BMW in the driveway. She hurried to her dresser and grabbed a blue ski sweater and matching socks, pulling them on as if she were in a fire drill. Sliding her feet into new wood-soled clogs, she clomped awkwardly down the stairs to meet him.

"I'll get it. I'll get it!" she called out as she ran. But it was too late. Heather had beaten her to the door.

"Ni-*cole*, it's your *date*," she sang in a smug, obnoxious singsong as Nicole reached the bottom stair. Heather stood with one hand on the doorknob, keeping Jesse on the stoop outside.

"Shut *up*, Heathen," Nicole whispered, resorting to the nickname her sister hated. "It's not a date."

"Oh, *no*," Heather retorted loudly. "That's why

163

you've been hogging the bathroom for an hour, putting on too much makeup."

Nicole felt her carefully made-up face go scarlet. She bounded to the door and snatched the doorknob from her sister. "You are *dead*," she whispered as she pushed past her. "Don't say I didn't warn you."

"Yeah, yeah . . . I'm real scared," Heather mocked.

Nicole stepped out onto the stoop and slammed the door, wondering how much Jesse had overheard. Their eyes met in the half-light of the front porch. He smiled, his amused expression saying it all.

"You *do* look nice," he offered.

"Don't pay attention to Heather," Nicole begged. "She's a total brat. I can't stand her."

Jesse rolled his eyes. "Don't worry. I have a stepsister that same age. Believe me, I know what you're going through. What is she, twelve?"

"Yeah."

Heather was thirteen—she'd have a *fit* to be mistaken for twelve. Nicole would have to be sure to tell her.

"Should we go?" Jesse asked, gesturing toward his car.

"Definitely."

Nicole followed Jesse to the waiting BMW, her heart fluttering with excitement. Aside from Heather's embarrassing little scene, it was practically a perfect evening. The night air held the chill of fall, and the moon was rising, sharp and bright. Jesse opened the passenger door, and Nicole slid into the luxurious black leather interior as if she'd been born to it.

Let this be the first date of many, she wished, crossing her fingers as Jesse walked around behind the car. *Well, okay, maybe it isn't a date, but it's close enough. It's a start. From here, who knows where things might go? Maybe he'll kiss me goodnight!* Her heart raced again, this time with hope.

Jesse opened the driver's door, dropped into his seat, and started the engine. "Well . . . Eight Prime, here we come," he said, rolling out of the driveway.

Nicole simply beamed as a brand-new thought occurred to her. She couldn't wait to see Eight Prime's faces when she and Jesse showed up at this meeting together!

Jenna paced nervously on the braided rug in the Conrads' den, bouncing between the front window and the snacks and drinks she'd set up on the coffee table. It was her first time hosting an Eight Prime meeting—Peter had held all the others—and she wasn't sure whether to be excited or afraid.

"Will you relax?" Peter said from the sofa. "You're starting to make *me* nervous."

"Here comes Ben!" she announced, ignoring his comment.

A late-model Chevy had stopped at the curb. Ben climbed out and waved to the driver. He was still on the sidewalk when Jesse's car appeared as well. Jesse and Nicole climbed out, Nicole looking dressy in tight new jeans.

"Jesse drove *Nicole*? How is Melanie getting here?" Jenna wondered aloud.

But her guests were already walking to the door, and she had to leave the window to let them in.

"Hey, Jenna!" Ben greeted her. "Cool house. What's to eat?"

Based on his extensive history of spilling things, Jenna was almost afraid to tell him, but she managed a fairly calm smile and pointed him toward the refreshments.

"How's it going?" Jesse asked casually, walking in behind him. Nicole was at Jesse's side, looking extremely pleased.

"Hi, Nicole. New pants?" Jenna asked.

Nicole tossed her blond hair and giggled. "Sort of."

Jenna wasn't sure why pants were funny, but she didn't have time to ask. Two more cars were pulling up: Leah with Miguel, and Melanie, driven by her father.

"Come on in. We're all here," Jenna called to the last three arrivals, struggling to ignore the fact that Leah and Miguel had arrived together again. Jenna had been so excited about having Miguel come to her house, taking pains to get the types of soda and chips he liked. Now she wondered why she'd bothered.

She led them to the den, where the rest of the group was gathered. Ben and Jesse were already working on the fruit plate, while Peter sampled the crackers and cheese. Jenna had bought Peter's favorite cheese, too—Gouda. She was glad now that she'd saved at least some of her budget for her friend.

"I like your house!" Nicole said brightly as Jenna entered the room. "Is it three stories? Or just an attic on top?"

"No, three stories. My bedroom's on the third floor." She said it proudly, enjoying the sound of the words *my bedroom*.

"Oh, how fun!" Nicole exclaimed. "You must have a killer view."

Jenna nodded. "It is pretty nice. Do you want to see it?" The offer was no sooner out of her mouth, though, than she remembered Melanie's incredible suite and wished she could take it back. She couldn't compete with a room like that—she didn't even want to try.

"Yes, let's!" said Nicole. "Let's all us girls go up!"

Great, Jenna groaned silently. Now she had to invite all the girls. And what was up with Nicole, anyway? She was acting way too cheerful.

"Sounds fun," said Leah. "Let's go."

"Sure. I'd like to see your room," Melanie agreed.

She sounded sincere, but Jenna thought she gave Nicole a weird look when she said it.

So it's not just me, Jenna thought. Nicole was frequently quiet to the point of seeming sulky. It was disconcerting to see her in such a good mood all of a sudden—and for no apparent reason.

Jenna put Peter in charge of entertaining the guys, and the four girls walked single file up the two flights of stairs to Jenna's room, Jenna in the lead. "Here we are," she said, pushing her door open wide and flipping on a light.

Everyone filed in, looking around and admiring her furniture. Jenna visualized Melanie's suite and dreaded the comparison. And yet . . . she had to admit that her room looked nice in the soft, gentle glow of the lamplight. And she liked the way she'd decorated, too, with her favorite posters and pictures. Instead of the expected sense that she didn't measure up, she felt a welcome rush of pride.

But then she remembered why they'd come. "Oops. I guess it's a little late to see the view," she apologized, gesturing toward the darkened window. "I should have realized." Instead of treetops, an image of four girls was reflected in the slightly rippled glass.

Nicole walked over and lifted the lower pane, bending forward to stick her head into the night, while Melanie and Leah sat on Jenna's bed and flipped through her magazines.

"I could see," Nicole said, bringing her head back inside and closing the window. "Enough to get the idea, at least. You must feel on top of the world up here."

"I do, kind of," Jenna admitted. She had, anyway, before she'd started comparing herself to Melanie. She dropped onto the double bed with Melanie and Leah, and Nicole sat down beside them.

"I wouldn't mind having this kind of space," Leah commented. "I love our condo, but it isn't very big. My room's about half this size."

"Mine's smaller, too," said Nicole. "*Plus* I have to share a bathroom with my little sister, and she comes through to bug me all the time."

Jenna glanced at Melanie, expecting her to fill them in on her private bath and walk-in closet. Melanie remained silent.

"I share a bathroom too," said Jenna. "But it's downstairs. I'm the only person on this floor."

"How nice!" Nicole sighed. "And you have your own phone!" She picked it up, pretending she had an important call. "Hel-looo!" she trilled. "I share my phone, too," she complained, putting it back down.

"I love your rug." Melanie pointed to the braided denim. "It makes the room feel cozy."

"Do you play guitar?" Leah asked before Jenna could respond. "I always wanted to learn, but I have no ear for music at all."

"*Peter* has no ear for music," Jenna corrected,

169

giggling. "Compared to him, our neighbor's basset hound is practically gifted."

"He can't be *that* bad," Melanie protested, a reproachful smile on her lips.

"Worse!" Jenna insisted happily. "Ask him if you don't believe me. He jokes about it himself."

The four of them laughed together, and Jenna was suddenly glad she'd invited them up. She'd been an idiot to worry about Melanie's room when her own was everything she'd wanted. So what if Melanie's house looked as if it belonged in a magazine? Jenna's was just as nice, in a homier, more realistic way. She looked around her now, completely satisfied again.

"You know, I just moved in here this weekend," she confided. "I was sharing a bedroom with my sister Maggie."

Melanie looked up with raised brows. "It sounds like you scored, then. This is a great room."

There wasn't the least touch of insincerity in the rich girl's voice. *Of course there isn't. This is a great room*, Jenna thought, feeling like a queen.

"Thanks. Well . . . I guess we'd better go back downstairs before the guys start the meeting without us."

"Good idea," said Nicole. "I don't want that crew deciding anything on its own. Leave it to Ben, and he'll have us giving pony rides in clown suits."

"Now *there's* an idea!" Leah teased. "I think you

170

ought to suggest it. Or, no—*piggyback* rides. That way we won't have to pay for the horses."

"As long as it's in clown suits, count me in," Melanie joked.

"Very funny," said Nicole. But all four of them were smiling as they trooped back down the stairs.

In the den, the guys had staked out seats and were waiting impatiently. Ben was sprawled in one of the cushy chairs, so Jenna took the other. Nicole and Leah sat between Jesse and Peter on the big couch, leaving Melanie with the spot next to Miguel on the short couch.

I could have sat there, Jenna realized too late.

She opened her steno pad and prepared to write notes, determined not to be depressed when only a moment before she had felt so good.

"Ben had an idea for the next fund-raiser while you were all upstairs," Peter told the girls.

The four of them looked at each other with horrified expressions, then burst into fits of laughter.

"What?" Ben protested.

"Just tell us it doesn't involve ponies or clown suits and we'll be okay," Leah said, still chuckling.

Ben looked confused. "Of course no ponies. I suppose someone *could* wear a clown suit, but I don't think it would be very scary."

The girls laughed convulsively, helpless to stop.

"I do," Melanie gasped.

"What's the matter with all of you?" Peter asked

disapprovingly, looking from one to the other. "You don't even know what the idea is yet."

"That's true," said Jenna, feeling a little guilty. "We're sorry, Ben. Go ahead."

Ben hesitated.

"Yes, Ben," Leah urged. "We're sorry. What did you have in mind?"

"A haunted house." He pushed back his limp blond bangs, then plunged ahead. "Peter said we made eleven hundred and twenty-eight dollars on the pumpkin sale. Since Halloween seems to be working for us, I thought we ought to stick with it."

"Eleven hundred dollars! That's good!" Nicole said.

Jenna nodded in agreement. Peter had told her their profit before the meeting, but it still sounded pretty impressive.

"There was this college-aged Christian group that used to do a huge haunted house in my neighborhood when I was little," Jesse said, smiling at the memory. "You should have heard the rumors that went around school every year before it opened—they made you put your hand in cow guts, they made you sit on a bench that gave electric shocks, there was a crazy guy with an ax pretending that he worked there. By the time my friends and I finally got inside, they could have shown *Bambi* and we'd have been terrified."

"Did they really give people shocks?" Ben asked, his eyes bugging behind his thick glasses.

"Of course not. Are you kidding? They'd have been sued blue. No, it was just a bunch of kids with overactive imaginations." Jesse sighed. "It was a blast."

"It does sound kind of fun," Jenna said.

"It does. But I'm not sure it's very feasible." Leah shot Ben an apologetic look. "I mean, for one thing, where would we hold it? We can't exactly have it in someone's garage."

There was silence while everyone thought that over.

"That *is* a problem," Jesse finally said. "That haunted house I was talking about—they used to do it in an enormous abandoned building. And it made a pretty big mess, too—what with the paint and fake blood and kids wetting their pants everywhere."

"Gross!" squealed Nicole. "Jesse!"

"I'm kidding." He chuckled, obviously pleased with his joke. "But it does make a mess."

"We'd need a bunch of props, too," Leah pointed out. "Even if we had a building, we'd have to build a ton of sets. We'd have to wire in sound effects and spooky lighting. Then there's costumes, tickets, advertising." She shook her head. "There's no way we could do all that with only eight people. Not only that, but we'd have to manage the line, sell tickets, guide kids through, act like spooks inside . . ." She trailed off, overwhelmed.

"I guess it's not a very good idea," Ben said. He looked crushed.

"No, it is," said Miguel. "It just might be too big for us."

"It would cost a lot to buy all that stuff," Melanie pointed out. "If we didn't get a good turnout, we could lose all the money we've made so far."

"Oh, no. We're not buying everything," Peter said decisively. "No way. But what if we got most of it for free?"

Jenna could tell by his tone that he had an idea. She gripped her pen more tightly, ready to write.

"There's nothing wrong with free," said Jesse. "What do you have in mind?"

"Well, the building's still a problem, but let's forget that for a minute. What if we ask the CCHS drama department to help with the props and costumes? When they find out the bus we're buying is to honor Kurt, they might lend us a bunch of stuff. We could even get some volunteers that way. And speaking of volunteers, I know my parents would chaperone and take tickets—we could *all* ask our parents to help. Don't forget about Chris and Maura and their college friends, either. Between them and us, we ought to know plenty of people."

Jesse nodded. "You're making it sound almost doable."

"We'd still have to buy some stuff," Peter acknowledged, "but probably not that much. And if we advertise, and run the haunted house three or four nights in a row . . ."

"I'll bet we could get five dollars a ticket," Ben piped up.

"Five dollars!" Jenna exclaimed. "Do you really think so?"

"I don't see why not," said Melanie. "The big ones in St. Louis get more like ten. I know those are professional, but ours is for charity, and that ought to count for something. If we—"

"If we got a couple hundred people a night, at five dollars a head," Jenna interrupted, carried away by the idea, "that would be—"

"A lot of money," Nicole interrupted in turn. "A whole lot more than we've made so far. I think we ought to do it."

"Maybe we *are* ready for something a little bigger," Leah mused.

"But what about the building?" asked Miguel.

Silence descended again. Everyone liked the idea now, but they still needed a place to do it.

"There's got to be somewhere," Jenna said, thinking aloud. "Maybe someone's parents know someone with a building we could use. If not, we could ask around at church this Sunday."

"It's worth a try," Peter said. "We should at least ask before we give up."

Everyone nodded.

"So now you *like* my idea!" Ben said triumphantly.

"I still don't know what it has to do with ponies, though," he added a second later.

"*Forget* the ponies, Ben," said Nicole. "It wouldn't be funny if we explained it now."

Ben shrugged, then brightened again. "Hey!" he said, turning to Melanie. "You know who you ought to ask to help us? Angela Maldonado. I gave her my hat at the pumpkin sale. Maybe she could wear that and come dressed up as a pumpkin." He seemed to think that over a moment, a dreamy smile on his face. Then he came back to the business at hand. "Myself, I'm going to be something scary. Dracula, or a werewolf or something."

"Maybe we can sell lemonade and let you pour," Melanie said, a wry smile on her face.

Jenna giggled to remember what a mess Ben had made of that task at Kurt Englbehrt's carnival. "That ought to be scary enough for anyone!"

Twelve

"Hello?" said Nicole, grabbing the cordless phone she shared with Heather out of its cradle on the bathroom counter. She hated keeping it there, and they had to be careful not to get it wet, but it was the only place they could both agree on. Besides, it was better than searching for it under the piles of laundry in Heather's room.

"Nicole? Hi. It's Jenna."

"Hi, Jenna," Nicole replied tentatively. She'd seen Jenna at lunchtime earlier that Friday, along with Courtney and Leah, and tomorrow's trip to the U.S. Girls modeling contest in St. Louis had been planned down to the last detail. Jenna calling her now wasn't a good sign.

"I've got some bad news and some good news," Jenna opened. "My parents aren't going to let me go to St. Louis."

"Why not?" cried Nicole. "I thought it was all set."

"So did I," Jenna said glumly. "But before, when they said I could go, for some reason they assumed

177

your parents were driving. With this storm coming in, my mom thought they'd cancel the trip. Then she found out it was just us girls going and she changed her mind. It's nothing personal—they wouldn't have let me go with any teenage driver."

Nicole tried to keep the disappointment out of her voice. "We'll miss you. I wish you could have come." Nicole didn't care if it rained from now until they left the next day—nothing would keep her from this contest.

"Me too. But wait, I haven't told you the good news yet."

"Oh, yeah. I forgot."

"I felt bad about asking for a seat in the car and then not going—especially when you didn't have enough room before to invite Melanie along. So I called her, and she's going to take my place! I told her you'd pick her up at eight, since that was when you were coming for me."

"Eight?" Nicole repeated in a strangled voice. Not having room in the car was just a lame excuse she'd made up when Courtney had put her on the spot about bringing Melanie. She couldn't believe that Jenna had actually bought it.

"Yeah. She's looking forward to it."

Why? thought Nicole. As much as she didn't want Melanie to go, it was hard to believe the feeling wasn't mutual.

Then a truly awful possibility occurred to her.

"She's not entering the contest, is she?" she asked breathlessly.

"No. She said she's too short to model, but she likes that mall. I think it'll just be fun for her to go somewhere after being cooped up for so long. She's probably looking forward to the drive as much as anything."

"Oh. Okay." Nicole didn't know what else to say. "Thanks, Jenna." She hung up the phone in a daze.

"This is *horrible*!" she groaned. But what could she have said to Jenna? Jenna was so naive—so nice all the time. How could Nicole have explained how it felt to be jealous of another girl simply because some guy she had a crush on liked her better? Jenna couldn't possibly understand.

Walking back into her room, Nicole shut the bathroom door, then stood looking blindly at the clothes she'd laid out everywhere—possible choices for the next day's contest. "Maybe it won't be that bad," she muttered, trying to resign herself to the worst. "After all, Melanie and Jesse are over now."

I hope.

It did seem that way, though. Those two still weren't speaking to each other. Meanwhile, Jesse was paying all kinds of attention to Nicole. Nicole smiled at the recollection of riding home with him from the Eight Prime meeting the night before. He hadn't kissed her at the door, but he *had* hesitated a little. He could have been thinking about it. In any event, she was definitely making progress.

I don't have to like Melanie, but I guess I don't have to hate her anymore either. The world's most perfect blonde just wasn't as big of a threat these days. *Except that she's going to be on the sidelines in her cute little cheerleader outfit, watching Jesse's every move at the game tonight, and you're going to be here at the house, watching videos with Heather,* Nicole thought, disgruntled.

The rumble of distant thunder sounded ominously outside Nicole's bedroom window. She paused to listen. The sky had been threatening rain all day and, even though so far it had managed only gusts of wind and an occasional sprinkle, the storm Jenna's parents were worried about could blow in anytime. If it rained hard enough, the game would be canceled. Nicole imagined Melanie and the rest of the cheerleaders running from the field, shrieking as the rain pelted down on their ruined curls. She couldn't help it—the idea brought a smile to her lips.

I hope it pours, she thought.

"Pull yourself together," Jesse muttered, peering out his windshield at the darkening sky over CCHS. "Geez. You're acting like a total wimp."

He took a couple of deep breaths, trying to gather the courage to go into the gym and suit up for the Hickory Hills game, but he was so nervous he felt as if he might puke all over his black leather upholstery. He could *not* play the way he'd played for the past two weeks. Not tonight. Not again. Somehow he had to find the confidence, the ability, to go out on that field and play the way he had during the season opener.

"So much for praying for rain," he grumbled. The clouds that had been threatening to turn serious all day had stalled and now seemed to be retreating. The weather wasn't going to save him. He reached for the door handle, then stopped, his fingers barely touching the cool metal.

I can't go out there.

But he didn't have a choice. If he skipped the game, he'd be off the team. He didn't want to play Hickory Hills, but he also didn't want to never play again.

You only had one bad game, he reassured himself, trying to get some perspective. *No one cares about bad practices. Get out there and dominate tonight and everything will be forgiven.*

That actually sounded pretty good. For a second he felt calmer.

Get out there and suck, an unwelcome voice in his head echoed back, *and you can hand your position to Eric Spenser on a plate.*

The thought did nothing to soothe his frazzled nerves.

Glancing hurriedly around to make sure no one was watching, Jesse pulled a pint of vodka out of his glove compartment and took a few quick, furtive swallows. The liquor burned going down, but he hardly noticed anymore. It worked, and that was all he cared about. He began to return the half-full bottle to its hiding place, then changed his mind and dropped it into his gym bag instead.

If I embarrass myself tonight, I'll need that later.

"Ouch," breathed Melanie, averting her eyes from the field as the crowd groaned. Jesse had just dropped another pass—his second.

"You stink, Jones!" an unsympathetic onlooker shouted from the stands.

Melanie wondered if Jesse had heard him. Sitting by herself on the cheerleaders' bench, she was hearing a lot of that type of thing.

I wonder what's the matter, she thought. Jesse had started out fine the first couple of plays, but then he'd dropped a pass. The mistake had seemed to rattle him—probably more than it should have—and ever since, he'd been playing terribly. He was in the wrong place half the time, and the rest of the time he was crashing into his teammates like a bull in a china shop. *He looks like he's not even sure why he's out there.*

The Wildcats lined up again, Jesse staggering through several more plays. Melanie couldn't understand what was happening. She'd have thought Jesse far too vain to ever look so pathetic in public. *This has got to be killing him*, she realized, feeling a twinge of pity. *There's no way he's doing it on purpose*.

She glanced up at the scoreboard. The third quarter was nearly over, and the Wildcats were only ahead by one point. The game was going to be close—too close for what should have been an easy win. Melanie, who had never much cared about football before, felt a dull, anxious ache in the pit of her stomach. If the Wildcats lost, would they blame their defeat on Jesse?

"Let's hustle!" Coach Davis screamed from the sideline, making her jump on the hard wooden bench. "Pay attention, for crying out loud!"

The Wildcats scrambled into position, waiting for the snap. Their center hiked the ball to Hank. For a moment everything was confusion. Then the Mustangs blitzed, rushing the quarterback for all they were worth. Hank dropped back in the pocket, trying to avoid the sack.

Oh, no. He's going down, Melanie worried.

A huge tackler dove forward and caught CCHS's quarterback by the waist, pulling him to the ground. Hank fell, but as he did he fired the ball skyward, far down the field. It was a Hail Mary pass—the kind where the whole team prays one of them will catch it. The ball sailed over the heads of Mustangs and Wildcats alike.

No one's going to catch that, Melanie predicted. The only person who even had a chance was a Mustang stationed halfway between everyone else and the end zone.

Then, out of nowhere, Jesse streaked down the field, his eyes fixed on the ball overhead. He was running like a madman—faster than she'd ever seen him go. He was gaining . . . he was almost there. . . . Could he?

He could! The ball dropped from the sky into his outstretched arms. The home crowd howled with excitement, jumping to its feet to cheer him on as he continued his race to the end zone. The lone Mustang defender was hard on his heels, but Jesse was ten yards from glory. Jesse was going to score!

And then the unthinkable happened. For no apparent reason, he lost control of the football. It squirted out of his arms like a grape popping free of its skin. Jesse lunged forward to grab it again, caught his toe in the sod, and fell facedown in the grass. The ball tumbled to the turf and began to roll.

Melanie watched, stunned, as the Mustang defender dashed forward. Reaching the ball just two yards short of the Wildcats' end zone, he scooped it up, then turned and sprinted back down the field. The visiting fans in the "away" bleachers erupted into utter pandemonium.

There was pandemonium on the field as well.

The Wildcats were completely unprepared for such a rapid turn of events. No one was in position to block the ball carrier—no one was even at that end of the field except Jesse, and Jesse was down. His teammates seemed momentarily frozen in place, stupefied into watching the runner gain ground, before they desperately charged the ball carrier, converging on him from points all over the field. But the Mustang was picking up blockers now, and picking up speed as well. He barreled through the Wildcats like a bowling ball through pins, barely altering his course as he ran straight up the field and into his end zone. The visiting crowd cheered wildly, making the bleachers ring. The Mustangs had just scored a touchdown off of Jesse's unforced fumble.

The field erupted too as the Mustangs reveled in their good fortune. Melanie stood still amid the clamor, unable to believe how the play had turned out. It would have been better if Jesse had never run for that sky ball, if he had let the pass drop incomplete. Because of him, the Wildcats were now down by five.

Then the Mustangs booted in the kick for the extra point and their lead increased to six.

"Jones!" Coach Davis bellowed hoarsely, waving Jesse off the field. A fresh player with *Spenser* on his jersey darted eagerly onto the grass, and Melanie knew Jesse was being replaced.

Poor Jesse, she thought as he shuffled to the bench. He sank down onto it, slumping over with his elbows on his thigh pads and his helmeted head in his hands. *He must feel awful.*

She felt an unexpected urge to sneak across the short distance between the cheerleaders' bench and the football players', to try to cheer him up.

Not that he's probably in the mood to talk to me. Aside from that single perfunctory visit to the hospital, he hadn't spoken to her once since their fight before her accident. For that matter, he hadn't spoken to her at the hospital, either. Melanie chewed her full bottom lip, wishing she hadn't been quite so harsh. The truth was, she kind of missed him. She wished they'd never had that fight.

She had just been sick to death of Jesse following her around, trying to score like some clueless wannabe Romeo. And it hadn't helped that most of the school seemed to think they were a couple. She'd desperately wanted to make their non-relationship clear, to put some distance between them. She still did. Just maybe not this much.

Melanie glanced his way again, then over at Coach Davis. *The coach'll have a coronary if he catches me and Jesse talking. Besides, what would I say?*

She stayed on the edge of her bench, trying to

make up her mind. Just then a roar from the crowd snapped her attention back to the field. The Wildcats had scored. She'd been so wrapped up in her thoughts, she hadn't even noticed they were close. The coach ran down the sideline to bellow about the extra kick, and Melanie saw her chance.

Pushing off her bench, she duckwalked forward to Jesse's, keeping her body low. "Cheer up," she said softly to his slumped-over back. "We just tied the score."

Jesse looked up in time to see the kick for the extra point sail between the goalposts.

"Even better," she corrected. "We're ahead."

Jesse turned to stare at her, his expression registering disbelief. "What are you doing here? I thought you were mad at me."

Melanie shrugged. "I guess I got over it."

"You sure have lousy timing. Everyone else is just getting into it."

"Oh, please," she scoffed. "So it's not your night. Big deal. We're still going to win, and you'll play better next time."

Jesse's blue eyes widened, then glazed over. "They won't even let me on the field next time. This is it. I'm finished." He dropped his head back into his hands.

"Don't be ridiculous. You're practically their star player."

"Are you making fun of me?" he asked without raising his head.

"Jesse! You caught that impossible pass, didn't you? If that other guy—"

"This isn't a coffee klatch, ladies!" an angry voice roared a short distance behind them.

Melanie jumped up, startled.

"We're supposed to be playing football, not exchanging gossip!" Coach Davis shouted, aiming a truly nasty look in their direction.

Jesse groaned loudly, again without raising his head, and Melanie slunk hurriedly back to the cheerleaders' bench.

Great, she thought. *Now I got him in trouble, too.*

Jesse fiddled with his shoelaces, the last player in the locker room. He still couldn't believe he'd fumbled—not when he'd had it in the bag like that. He didn't even know what had happened. The Wildcats had managed to maintain their one-point lead to win the game, but afterward, in the showers, no one had so much as looked his way. Not even his so-called friends, Gary Baldwin and Barry Stein. If he'd made that touchdown, he'd have been a hero. Instead, he was the biggest loser on the team.

He shook his head, as if he could wake himself out of the nightmare he'd somehow stumbled into. First a dropped pass, then a fumble . . . the way he was playing didn't seem possible. It didn't even seem real.

Oh, it's real, all right, he told himself, rising slowly to his feet. *You suck.* He reached to open his locker and grab his gym bag, but before his hand touched the door a voice spoke up at the end of the row.

"What you need," Coach Davis advised, walking toward him, "is to settle down. You're wound so tight I'm surprised you don't snap. You need to settle down and find that groove you were in before." The coach's voice was hoarse from shouting, but his tone was calm and friendly.

Jessie latched on to the man's words like a life preserver. "I—I know," he stammered. "I just don't understand why everything's going so wrong for me all of a sudden."

"This isn't about you, Jones. It's about a *team.* We all win or lose together. You need to stop thinking the entire fate of the Wildcats rests on your shoulders, and you *absolutely* need to stop playing that way. Stop worrying about being the star, and start thinking about contributing to the team."

"You're right," Jesse agreed quickly, thrilled that the coach hadn't written him off completely. "It's just that I'm not sure what I can do differently. I mean, I'm trying really hard—"

"You're trying *too* hard. That's my point. Lighten up a little. Have some fun."

"Lighten up? Are you sure? I feel like I ought to be practicing twice as much or something."

"Listen, Jesse." It was practically unheard of for the coach to use a player's first name. "I've seen players self-destruct under pressure before. You probably think you're the first guy ever to fumble while running, but it happens all the time. A guy starts thinking about where he's going, instead of about where he is. . . . I think you have talent, a lot of promise, but you have to try to relax out there."

Jesse took a deep breath and forced himself to sound calm. "I will."

"Good. And don't worry about Spenser. I like the kid, but I'm not in a hurry to replace you. You'll get your chance to prove yourself."

Coach Davis smiled and punched him lightly on the shoulder. Jesse's knees actually sagged. It was such a relief to know the coach didn't think he was a loser.

"Thanks, Coach," Jesse murmured. "You won't be sorry."

"I know." The coach pointed to Jesse's closed locker. "So what do you say you grab your stuff so the two of us can get out of here?"

"Oh. Right." Jesse turned toward his locker, a million things on his mind as his hand reached for the latch. *I'll pay Coach back for giving me this chance.* The locker door swung open. *I'll show him and everyone else at this school how good I can really be.*

They both saw it at the same time. The bottle of vodka Jesse had taken from his gym bag and stashed on the small upper shelf caught the harsh overhead light, reflecting it like a traitorous mirror.

"What the hell is that?" rasped the coach.

Thirteen

"Oh, wow," Nicole breathed, overwhelmed. She was standing at a metal railing with Courtney, Leah, and Melanie, looking down on the first-floor courtyard of the enormous Skyline Mall. The contest area spread beneath her, seemingly packed with thousands of gorgeous girls, all dressed in U.S. Girls jeans.

Courtney tossed her hair and laughed. "I tried to warn you this was a *national* contest," she said gleefully, obviously enjoying herself. "Of course, this is only the Missouri turnout. In some of the other *forty-nine* states, they probably got even *more* contestants. Don't worry, though, Nicole. I know they're only picking one girl here, but when you get to the finals in California, they're taking a whole big five."

"I feel sick," Nicole gasped.

Leah chuckled and leaned out over the rail. "If you aim right, you could knock out quite a bit of competition that way."

To Nicole's surprise, Melanie came to her rescue.

"You guys are awful," she said reproachfully. "Nicole must be nervous enough without that kind of help."

Nicole tried to smile her thanks, but her face was suddenly paralyzed. *I can't believe this*, she thought. *After everything I went through to get here* . . .

The actual drive had been surprisingly easy. The storm had rained itself out overnight, leaving their route sunny and mostly dry. But what about the dieting, the agonizing over her outfit, the begging of her parents, the stressing, the dreaming? It all seemed totally pointless, even ridiculous, now. Nicole looked down on that sea of girls and knew in her heart that she had no chance of winning. If she hadn't dragged her friends all the way to St. Louis, she wouldn't even have gone onstage.

"Shouldn't you be checking in or something?" Melanie asked, jolting Nicole back to the present. She pointed down to a serpentine line of girls filing past registration tables draped with white bunting. Beyond the tables were hundreds of folding white chairs and a stage with a modeling runway. "If the rest of us are going to get a seat, it looks like we'd better hurry," Melanie added. "Those chairs are already filling up."

Nicole nodded dizzily, and the four girls took an escalator down to the first level, where they joined the long line. It took forever to move to the front, but Nicole was so nervous, it seemed like only a minute. Her eyes darted distractedly over the other would-be models in their red-white-and-blue out-fits while her friends chatted and Courtney made catty comments about the rare unattractive contestant. Finally it was Nicole's turn.

"Name?" a woman behind the table asked curtly.

"Uh, Nicole Brewster. I preregistered."

"Wait here." The woman turned to a smaller table behind her, walked to a box marked *A–D*, and flipped through it until she found a large card with Nicole's name. Returning with the card, she pulled a thick envelope from under her table, opened it, and took out a set of three stickers, all with *314* marked on them in big black numerals. She peeled one of the stickers off its backing and affixed it to Nicole's card, then set the card in order on top of a growing pile.

"You'll be number 314," she said, handing Nicole the two remaining stickers and the rest of the contents of the envelope. "Put one of these stickers on your front and one on your back, and make sure they're where the judges can see them. You need to go to the backstage area." She gestured vaguely behind her. "They'll tell you what to do over there. Contest rules are in the envelope—you can read them while you wait."

Nicole nodded, took the envelope, and stepped away from the table.

"Name?" the harried woman asked Leah.

Leah drew back and laughed at the misunderstanding. "Thanks, but I'm with her," she said, pointing to Nicole. "I'm not competing."

The woman seemed surprised. She paused long enough to look Leah over, then shook her head and smiled. "Oh, honey, you really ought to. As tall and leggy as you are? Are you kidding me?"

"I'm not sure modeling's my thing," Leah said, looking down at her 501 Levi's and loose white button-down shirt. "Besides, I didn't sign up, I didn't bring other clothes—"

The registrar shoved a blank card at her. "Not a problem. All you do is fill this out."

Leah hesitated.

"I think you'd do well," the woman urged.

To her surprise, Nicole found herself joining in. "Please, Leah? It'll be much more fun if you come with me." Neither of them was going to win—that much was obvious now—but if Leah competed, at least Nicole would have someone to hang out with backstage. "Please?" she repeated.

"I don't know. . . ."

"Oh, go on, Leah," Melanie chimed in. "What have you got to lose?"

"My self-respect?" Leah ventured. The others shook their heads.

"Just do it," Courtney said. "What the heck."

"Please?" Nicole begged once more.

Leah shrugged, beaten. "Oh, all right. If it will really make you happy."

Melanie wriggled in the hard folding chair, trying to get comfortable. The loud dance-mix music pounded on her eardrums, doing its utmost to bring on a headache. Of all the boring things she'd ever sat through, the U.S. Girls modeling contest was threatening to last the longest.

One by one the contestants came to the stage as their numbers were called. Then they walked to the end of the runway, posed, turned, and walked back again. Each girl got only twenty or thirty seconds—there were just so *many* of them.

"Now I know what they mean by a cattle call," Melanie told Courtney, leaning close to be heard over the music. "This thing is endless."

Courtney shook her head. "You're not kidding. I don't even know how they're going to pick someone. Everyone's starting to look the same."

It was true. After about the first hundred, Melanie's mind had glazed over. *All that red, white, and blue doesn't help*, she thought. *It's like watching a clone festival.*

The song that was playing finally ground to an end, and a new one started up. Melanie had long since lost track of how many of last year's songs she'd endured. On top of that, she was getting hungry. She was just wondering if she dared make a run to the food court when—

"Number 314—Nicole Brewster," the announcer droned over the music.

"Go, Nicole!" Courtney screamed like a loyal friend.

Melanie glanced up to see Nicole already onstage, walking toward the runway with stiff, frightened steps. "Yeah, Nicole!" she yelled.

Nicole looked cute in her jeans and a cropped red shirt, a red bandanna in her hair. Unfortunately, she also looked scared to death. She walked mechanically to the end of the runway, a wooden expression on her face, then seemed to remember to smile. When she tried, however, her terrified attempt looked more like a grimace. She turned and walked away more smoothly, her tight jeans emphasizing her slender figure, but Melanie already knew she wouldn't win. A quick glance at Courtney confirmed that she knew it too.

Poor Nicole, Melanie thought, feeling genuinely sorry for her. After all, it took a lot of courage to enter a contest, and Melanie didn't think Nicole was completely off base in her dream of being a model. She was thin enough, she had those shocking turquoise eyes . . . She just didn't have any presence, or poise, or whatever it was that made people sit up and take notice. Nicole had come and gone without a ripple. The next girl was already on the stage, then the next. It was as if Nicole had never been there.

"Number 318—Leah Rosenthal," droned the announcer.

"Go, Leah!" Melanie and Courtney called automatically.

Leah bounded through the backstage curtain, throwing the fabric wide where the other girls had slipped demurely through the opening. She headed straight for the runway, her head held high. In contrast to the other contestants, her clothes were casual to the point of making a statement, and she was wearing almost no makeup. Her brown hair swung rhythmically across her shoulders as she walked, completely free of barrettes, bandannas, or other red-white-and-blue accessories, and on her feet were plain white sneakers. She hadn't changed a single thing to cater to the judges.

She hit the runway confidently, even defiantly, taking long, sure strides on the polished wood. Her hazel eyes gazed out over the heads in the crowd, her full lips curving slightly, as if she knew a joke she wasn't going to tell them. Melanie felt herself sitting up in her chair. Whatever indefinable quality had been lacking in Nicole, Leah had enough for them both.

"Oh, my God, she's *good*!" Melanie said, staring at this completely unexpected new Leah.

"She knows how to work an attitude, that's for sure," Courtney agreed. "I've never seen anyone look less like they cared in my life."

"I don't think she *does* care."

"Whatever. It's working."

And Melanie and Courtney weren't the only ones who thought so. All over the audience, people were sitting up straighter in their chairs, talking to each other. A group of local guys catcalled loudly, and there was even a spontaneous scattering of applause from the otherwise sleepy crowd.

Leah acted as if none of it mattered. She reached the end of the runway, stopped and glanced at the judges, then turned and strode off like a woman with somewhere to go. She pushed back through the curtain without the slightest break in momentum.

"Number 319—Annie Edwards." Even the announcer sounded a little more awake.

Courtney shook her head, her usually cynical eyes full of admiration. "I'm glad *I'm* not going onstage after that."

Leah trotted down the short, wobbly staircase at the back of the makeshift stage, relieved that her turn was over. The whole idea of being in a modeling contest was ridiculous—she'd never have done it if Nicole hadn't begged her.

"How did you do?" Nicole asked anxiously as Leah reached firm ground. "How did it go?"

Leah shrugged. "I walked to the end. I walked back. Not much to it."

"Leah!" Nicole protested, obviously wanting details. "I was so terrified I thought I'd pass out. Weren't you scared?"

"Well . . . not really." Leah didn't want to hurt Nicole's feelings, but she thought modeling was kind of lame. She supposed someone needed to do it, but it didn't have to be her. She knew she wasn't going to win the contest—she didn't *want* to win the contest. That left her with nothing to be afraid of except being spotted by someone she knew.

"I wish I could have seen you walk," Nicole said. "I couldn't see anything down here."

"I know. I couldn't see you, either." The two of them had ended up a few numbers apart because Leah had let people go ahead of her in line while she filled out her entry form. As a result, each of them had been on the ground while the other one was onstage. "We should have brought a camera so Melanie and Courtney could tape you."

Nicole groaned. "I'm glad we didn't. I was terrible."

Leah laughed. "How terrible could you be? You walk up and down a runway. It's not brain surgery."

Leah had meant her comment to be funny, but Nicole wasn't smiling. "I just . . . choked," she said, the beginnings of tears pooling in her eyes. "I was so scared. I totally froze."

"So . . . hey," Leah soothed, putting an arm around her. "Stuff like that happens to every-

200

one. Besides, I'll bet you did better than you think."

"Really?" Nicole asked, looking at her hopefully.

"Sure. Let's go find Melanie and Courtney and see what they thought."

"We're supposed to stay back here until they announce the winner," Nicole reminded her. The contestants were confined to a large, roped-off area that started behind the stage and extended back into the mall.

Leah stifled a groan. "Do you really want to stay that long?" She couldn't exactly tell Nicole she was hoping to get home in time to see Miguel that evening, but that was her plan.

"Don't you?" Nicole asked, surprised.

"Well, not really. We've already been here for hours, and when this thing breaks up, everyone's going to be leaving at once. If we go now, we can miss the rush."

"But it's almost over!" Nicole protested, pointing to the short line of girls still waiting to go onstage. "I want to see who wins."

"All right." Leah wasn't sure why it mattered, but she supposed Nicole was curious to see who had beat her out. She leaned against a rail at the edge of the backstage area, determined to wait patiently.

They had only been there a few minutes when a beautiful girl walked up to them, wearing the standard red-white-and-blue outfit. "I was right behind you onstage," she told Leah coldly. "Thanks for ruining my confidence."

"Wh-What?" Leah stammered.

The girl broke into a friendly smile, her perfect white teeth contrasting with flawless brown skin. "Just kidding. You were great."

"Me?" Leah didn't know what to say. "Uh, thanks."

"How long have you been modeling?" the other girl asked.

"*Me*? Oh, no. I've never modeled. This was just kind of a last-minute fluke."

The girl raised her eyebrows. "Well, I've modeled a lot, and you could have fooled me. Good luck, all right?"

"Yeah. You too," Leah said. The other girl walked away.

"Leah!" Nicole burst out immediately. "Aren't you excited?"

Not exactly, Leah thought, forcing herself not to look at her wristwatch.

At last the line of remaining contestants dwindled to a few girls, then to none. The audience burst into applause that sounded more relieved than enthusiastic as the final girl left the stage. Leah started sliding along the back of the crowd, still leaning on the railing. She wanted to be as close to the exit as possible, so that she could bail the moment the winner was announced.

A comedian of sorts took the stage, attempting to elicit a response from the restless crowd while the judges tallied their results. *How long can it take?* Leah thought impatiently. *They're using computers.*

The comedic patter droned on, occasionally punctuated by mercy laughs from the audience. Leah was right at the exit now, Nicole at her side. She strained to see around the end of the stage, looking for Melanie and Courtney. If she could make eye contact, she could at least get them moving toward their exit too. She had just spotted them when a new voiced boomed out over the loudspeakers.

"Ladies and gentlemen! On behalf of the U.S. Girls Clothing Company, it gives me great pleasure to announce our winner, who, in addition to taking the title here today, will receive an all-expenses-paid trip for four to compete in our national finals in Hollywood, California."

A hush fell over the crowd.

"Won't you put your hands together," the announcer continued, "for one of hottest, one of the freshest new faces we've seen this season? Ladies and gentlemen, give it up for Missouri's newest U.S. Girl—Ms. *Leah Rosenthal!*"

Fourteen

"I'm really sorry, Nicole," Leah apologized again in the car on the long drive home. "I never dreamed I might actually win. I'll drop out."

Nicole took her eyes off the road long enough to glance at Leah's two dozen red and white roses, tied with a wide blue ribbon. She still couldn't believe Leah had accidentally won the contest—*her* contest. There was no denying she felt cheated.

Still . . . it's not Leah's fault. You're the genius who begged her to enter.

And it *was* nice of Leah to offer to drop out of the finals just to make her feel better. Nicole had a feeling she'd do it, too.

She took a deep breath. "Don't even think of dropping out," she said. "We're all really proud of you."

"Totally," Courtney put in from the backseat. "I mean, no offense, but what were the odds?"

"You *deserved* to win, Leah," said Melanie. "When they called your name and you came walking out, it was like you owned the stage or something. The entire audience noticed. All the other girls came out expecting us to look at them, but when you came out it was totally different—like you were there to look at *us*."

"You ruled," Courtney said in summation.

"I wish I could have seen it," Nicole said wistfully. Leah had always seemed so down-to-earth to her. Pretty, but not a head-turner. The girl Melanie and Courtney were describing sounded like someone Nicole didn't even know.

"I wish I'd never gone out there," Leah said. "I'm going to call U.S. Girls as soon as we get home and tell them they made a mistake. They'll have to pick somebody else."

"No!" Nicole cried. "I mean, please don't, Leah. It's not like I came in second or anything." Actually, they'd announced two runners-up after Leah's victory walk, meaning Nicole hadn't come in third, either, but everyone was being awfully nice about not mentioning that. "I'm *glad* you won. Really." It wasn't even that big of a lie, she realized to her surprise.

"Do you mean it?" Leah asked uncertainly.

"Sure. If I couldn't win myself, having you win is the next-best thing. Hey, and you know," she added slowly, "in a way I'm even *responsible* for you winning. If it wasn't for me, you never would have been there in the first place."

"That's absolutely true," Leah said. "I don't know whether to thank you or kick you."

Melanie and Courtney laughed.

"Very funny," said Nicole. "I made you practically famous, is all."

"And you're positive that's a *good* thing?"

"Of course! You'll be thanking me in January, when the rest of us are freezing our butts off in Clearwater Crossing and you're in sunny California."

"*If* I decide to go."

"Leah! You have to!" Nicole insisted.

"She's right," Melanie agreed. "Why would you pass up a free trip to Hollywood? Hey, and who will you take with your other three tickets?"

"My parents and . . . I don't know. Maybe my grandmother."

"If your parents wouldn't mind, I'm half tempted to go with you," Melanie told her.

"Really?" Leah turned around in the front seat. "Are you serious?"

Nicole saw Melanie shrug in the rearview mirror. "Maybe. My dad would probably let me. I could ask for the money for Christmas."

"What a blast that would be!" Courtney said. "Can you imagine if we *all* went? Beaches, shopping, movie stars . . . we'd be the queens of CCHS."

"Maybe Jenna could go too," Melanie said. "It *would* be fun."

"And just think if you win in the finals, Leah!" Nicole jumped in, carried away. "You'll have your

206

picture everywhere—malls, magazines, even on billboards!"

Leah's eyes widened with alarm. "You are *not* convincing me, Nicole."

"Oh, stop being so modest," said Courtney. "Melanie and I sat in that stupid mall till our butts fell asleep for you. The least you can do is give us an excuse to go to California."

Jenna turned up her radio and sang as she worked on a project for her textiles class. Church that morning had been especially inspiring, and the new song the choir performed had gone perfectly. It was always a great feeling to sing well in church, to know she had done her best with the talent God had given her. Not only that, but everyone had said nice things afterward and asked if they'd made much money on the pumpkin sale. People were already promising to support the haunted house if Eight Prime went through with that.

Jenna put down her colored pencil and studied her project critically. She was supposed to be designing a theater costume for a play of her choice. That meant making a colored drawing of the costume and stapling snippets of the various fabrics to be used along its edge. After much indecision, she had finally decided to do a dress for the role of Christine Daaé in *The Phantom of the Opera*. She wanted to do something fancy, to be worn in a

207

scene where the young singer performs at the Paris Opera House. So far it looked pretty good, but it still needed something. . . .

"I wonder if Sarah used up those gold and silver markers she made her Christmas cards with last year," Jenna said, thinking aloud. A little metallic paint could go a long way toward making her design look more glamorous, more like a real opera costume. "I could draw in some gold braid and sequins." She pushed back her chair and got up, intent on finding the pens.

She ran down the two flights of stairs to Sarah's room and was about to walk in without knocking when she heard a strange sound from within. She froze, her hand barely touching the knob. Was Sarah crying? She was! Her sister's brokenhearted sobs came through the door despite her obvious attempts to muffle them.

What could be wrong? Jenna wondered, worried. Even though she was the youngest, Sarah almost never cried. It was far more common for Maggie to blubber, or Allison, or, much as she hated to admit it, Jenna herself. Besides, Jenna had seen Sarah from her window not an hour before, playing in the backyard with a friend, and she'd seemed perfectly fine then. Afraid that Sarah had somehow gotten hurt, Jenna turned the knob and charged into the room.

"Caitlin!" she gasped.

Her older sister sat up quickly, a frantic look in her streaming eyes. She wiped her face, then, apparently realizing it was hopeless, turned her back instead. "What are you doing in here?" she said in a shaking voice. "Can't you knock?"

"I—I'm sorry," Jenna stammered. "I thought you were Sarah."

Caitlin made no answer, apparently waiting for Jenna to leave, but Jenna hesitated in the doorway. She hadn't seen Caitlin cry in years. Something terrible must have happened.

"Caitlin, what's the matter? Can't I help?"

Caitlin shook her head mutely, her back still to the door.

Jenna took a few steps into the room, craning to see her sister's face. "Do you want me to go get Mom?"

No answer.

"Dad?"

"Please don't. Just go."

"Caitlin . . . ," Jenna began, but before she got any further, her sister threw herself down on the bed, sobbing like a little girl.

"I'm such a failure!" she said through her tears. "I can't do anything right."

"What are you talking about?" Jenna asked, rushing to her sister's side. She perched on the edge of Caitlin's bed, leaning down to bring her face closer. "That's not true!"

"Yes, it is," Caitlin insisted miserably. "Look at me. I'm eighteen and I still live at home."

"But I thought you *wanted* to live at home. At least, you know . . . until you get a job."

Jenna's comment only sent her sister into fresh agony. "What kind of loser wants to room with her ten-year-old sister?" she wailed. "Do you think I don't know how pathetic I am?"

At a loss, Jenna hesitatingly put a hand on her sister's back, stroking it gently. Caitlin continued to cry, while Jenna wished their mother would come. Mrs. Conrad always knew exactly what to do to make everyone feel better. Jenna tried to guess what her mom would say.

"Cat, why don't you go to college?" she asked at last, hoping she wasn't too far off. "You can always get a job later, when you graduate."

"I'm *never* going to get a job!" Caitlin lifted her face out of her pillow long enough to grab a thick stack of envelopes from the nightstand and shove them at Jenna. "There's the proof if you don't believe me."

Jenna took the letters and stared down at them uncomprehendingly. They were all business envelopes addressed to Ms. Caitlin Conrad. "I don't understand."

"They're 'thanks anyway' letters. From all the places I've applied to." Caitlin sat up and sniffed defiantly. "Dear Ms. Conrad," she mocked, as if she were reading. "Thank you for interviewing with us. We regret to inform you that we wouldn't hire you if you were the last person left on Earth."

The rare show of spunk shocked Jenna almost as much as the tears, but what came out of her mouth was, "You've been interviewing?"

"Of course I've been interviewing! What did you think—that I watch soaps all day and practice my needlepoint? I just didn't want everyone to know, because nothing ever comes from it."

She collapsed back onto her pillow, crying inconsolably. "I *should* have gone to college. I just couldn't face another school . . . a big new campus full of strangers. No, I thought I'd stick close to home and get a nice safe job instead."

Caitlin drew in a sloppy, shuddering breath. "But I'm terrible in interviews. *Terrible!* Someone asks me a question and my hands sweat and my voice shakes, and I can barely say hello. I'm such an idiot! No one is ever going to hire me. And I just can't face going out there and getting turned down again." Tears threatened to drown out her voice altogether. "I can't do it anymore."

"Then don't," Jenna urged, not knowing what else to say. "Give yourself a break for a while."

"A *break?* What am I on right now? All the people I went to high school with are off at college, making lives for themselves, and I'm just a big loser living in her parents' house with a ten-year-old roommate!"

Caitlin continued to sob while Jenna rubbed ineffectually at her back. "Maybe . . . well, maybe you should try not to be so shy, Caitlin."

"I *have* tried, Jenna! Do you think I *like* it? I don't know why God had to make me this way. Why can't I be like the rest of you?

Jenna shook her head. She desperately wanted to help, but she didn't know what to say, what to do. And then she realized something else.

I made this happen.

The knowledge made her feel even worse. *If I'd left things alone, at least Caitlin would still have her own room.* Jenna was ashamed to remember the way she had badgered, constantly agitating for Caitlin to get a job, when all the time her sister had been trying unsuccessfully to do just that.

And her precious new room, the one she'd fought so hard for . . . it was obvious now that Caitlin had been doing her best to give it to her all along. Jenna had thought her sister so selfish, so oblivious, but now she saw that Caitlin must have been worrying about it every day—more than Jenna, even. No wonder she'd finally offered to move in with Sarah.

If I'd only been a little more patient, Jenna thought, *maybe Caitlin wouldn't have felt like she had to turn the room over right away. And then maybe she wouldn't have lost hope. I'm the one who was selfish. And clueless, too. Poor Caitlin.*

Jenna knew what she had to do. She did it quickly, before she could change her mind.

"Listen, Cat," she said, hugging her sister. "You know what? You take your old room back, and I'll move in with Sarah."

Caitlin shook her head, still sobbing.

"Come on," Jenna insisted, feeling guiltier by the second. "I want to trade back."

"I don't. A loser like me doesn't deserve her own bedroom."

"You're *not* a loser, Cat. You're just having a little hard time. Don't worry, though—I'm going to help you. Okay?"

Caitlin glanced up, her eyes swollen with crying. "I wish I knew how."

Jenna only nodded reassuringly. She could hardly tell Caitlin that she wished she knew, too.

Fifteen

"Well? Do you have anything to say?" Principal Kelly leaned back in his fake leather desk chair, his dark eyes fixed on Jesse's blue ones.

Jesse shifted uncomfortably. "No."

"No, what?" Jesse's father prompted sharply.

"Uh . . . no, sir. I don't."

"Do you deny any of what Coach Davis has told me?"

"No. Sir."

The principal shook his head. "You leave me no choice, Jesse. You're suspended from school for a week, beginning this morning, and you're off the Wildcats indefinitely. It's up to the coach whether you'll be allowed to rejoin the team."

Jesse nodded mutely. He'd expected it. All weekend long, in fact, he'd been preparing for the worst. He'd been so afraid of losing his composure, of breaking down and appearing weak, that now he just felt numb. He couldn't sustain that level of emotion anymore. It was almost as if nothing had happened at all, or as if it had happened to someone else.

As it turned out, Dr. Jones was the one who lost his composure. "I hope you're proud of yourself!" he exploded. "Your mother and I couldn't be more humiliated."

My mother—that's a hot one, Jesse thought, not for the first time. *Poor Elsa won't be able to show her face at the country club with her fellow leeches.*

"Well, that's all I have to say," the principal concluded calmly. "We'll see you in school next Monday, Jesse, but I hope to never see you in this office again. You've been a good student until now. It's time to get back on track."

Out of the groove. Off the track. That's turning into the story of my life.

Jesse rose from his chair and extended his hand to Principal Kelly, to show there were no hard feelings. He couldn't trust his voice, but at least he could make that gesture.

The principal shook his hand warmly. "Turn it around, son," he urged. "I have confidence in you."

Yeah, right, Jesse thought bitterly. After all, the guy was still kicking him out of school. But at least he *said* he had confidence. That was more than Jesse's father had done.

"I can't believe you got into this mess," Dr. Jones berated him as the two of them left the main building and walked to his silver Mercedes. He'd parked in the teachers' lot, in total disregard of the many signs. "We raised you better than that. I can't believe you could be so stupid."

Jesse climbed into the big car silently, wondering who "we" was and what exactly his father thought was stupid—drinking or getting caught. Coming from a man who threw back a couple before dinner every night, the comment seemed hypocritical.

"You're grounded. That goes without saying," Dr. Jones declared, starting the engine.

But you're saying it anyway.

"And while you're hanging around home on your *vacation* this week, I have a few projects for you. You can start by mowing and edging the lawn. Then I want you to pull every weed on the property. *Every* weed—I'm going to check."

Jesse watched the town slip by outside his window. The Joneses had an enormous house, surrounded by an equally enormous lawn. They also had a gardener. His father's assignment was strictly busywork, something to punish him further. Besides, wouldn't it be snowing or something soon in this godforsaken place? Who cared about the stupid lawn when it was about to freeze anyway?

"After that, you can get started on the toolshed. It needs to be painted. You'll have to strip all the old paint first. . . ."

Jesse tuned him out. The toolshed was pretty much the last thing on his mind just then. He was off the Wildcats—maybe for good. His stomach lurched sickeningly at the thought.

What were the people at school going to say? He was never going to live this down. Even if he got back on the team—even assuming he figured out how to play football again—people would always gossip about this disaster whenever his name came up.

And then there was Eight Prime. Would they kick him out of the group now, when they found out what he'd done? He wasn't exactly a role model for the Junior Explorers anymore—even he had to admit that.

Jesse thought about the last time he'd seen Jason, at Peter's church. The little boy's eyes had been wide with hero worship for Jesse, his adopted big brother, a real Wildcat. Jesse imagined the light going out in those eyes and swallowed hard. He couldn't face it.

He wasn't sure he could face any of it, really, but that, at least, he had a choice about.

He was dropping out of Eight Prime.

About the Author

Laura Peyton Roberts holds an M.A. in English literature from San Diego State University. A native Californian, she lives with her husband in San Diego.